Also by Natalie C. Parker

The Devouring Wolf

— YOUNG ADULT NOVELS —

The Seafire Series
Seafire
Steel Tide
Stormbreak

Beware the Wild
Behold the Bones

THE NAMELESS WITCH

NATALIE C. PARKER

RAZORBILL

RAZORBILL

An imprint of Penguin Random House LLC, New York

First published in the United States of America by Razorbill,
an imprint of Penguin Random House LLC, 2023

Text copyright © 2023 by Natalie C. Parker
Interior illustrations copyright © 2023 by Tyler Champion

Visit us online at PenguinRandomHouse.com.

Library of Congress Cataloging-in-Publication Data is available.

ISBN 9780593203989

Printed in the United States of America

1 3 5 7 9 10 8 6 4 2

BVG

Design by Tony Sahara
Text set in Averia Serif Libre Light

Cover art by Tyler Champion
Cover design by Jessica Jenkins

For Dhonielle and Zoraida,
my own wolf pack

PROLOGUE

NAMELESS

Once, there was a young witch who lived with her mother on the prairie. For a while, she was just like other witches. She did her lessons and her chores, and she never, ever used her magic in public.

Then one day, she changed.

An extraordinary spell filled her with more magic than she had ever touched. She became more powerful than any other witch on the continent, more powerful than her mother and her grandmother and her great-grandmother combined, and for a while it was like living in a dream.

Magic sang to her. She could hear it in her mother and in all the witches of her coven. They each had their own tune, and when they came together, the song they created was so unbearably beautiful that the girl would burst into tears, unable to explain that she wasn't sad but something else. Something beyond telling.

Her mother didn't understand.

"You hear us?" she'd asked, with a frown of concentration. She had frowned more and more often since the extraordinary spell had altered the girl, so the girl was very careful with her questions.

"I hear all magic," she'd explained. She heard other things, too, but she didn't want to make her mother frown any harder. "Does that mean *you* don't?"

"We don't," the girl's mother said, drawing a clear line between her daughter and other witches. Then she added, "You'll have to get used to it. And until you do, you must be careful. You can't go around sobbing or giggling at nothing, or folk will get the wrong idea about you."

"You mean that I'm a witch?" the girl asked.

Her mother pressed her lips together and shook her head. "Worse," she said.

That hadn't made any sense to the girl. Being discovered as a witch was absolutely the most terrible thing that could happen to a person.

If her mother said there was something worse, the girl wanted to know what it was, but before she could ask, her mother thrust the cast-iron skillet into her hands and told her to prep the cornbread for dinner. The conversation was over.

The young witch had done her best. She practiced tuning out the melodic strains of other witches. She learned to identify the urgent songs of items that had been imbued with magic—they sounded like droning cicadas in the summertime, right up until the moment they burned out and went quiet again, leaving only crusty exoskeletons behind. She found that even people and things that weren't magical had their own resonance. The world was full of songs.

And they all rang through her.

Until the day she found a song that didn't.

She was waiting while her mother conducted business at the bank when she heard it: a song like two blades of grass whispering past one another, like the strike of flint against flint, the quiet hiss of a spark flashing to life.

It did not sound like witches. Witches sounded like rainstorms, with voices that sighed just as often as they crackled with laughter or thundered with conviction. Witch songs made her want to cry from the beauty of them.

This song made her want something else.

Power, sang a voice in her mind. She wasn't bothered by the voices, because they had come with the extraordinary spell that gave her all the songs. But she didn't always understand them. There were seven distinct voices, and she had a sense that some were older than others.

"What kind of power?" she asked, softly lest anyone think she was talking to herself, which she was.

Bone power, the same voice answered.

Intrigued, the witch followed the unusual whispering song toward the park, where she found a boy, not much older than she was. He had frosty-pale skin and dark brown hair, with eyes that reminded her of spring moss.

"What are you?" she'd asked, walking right up to him.

He'd stumbled back, with a disbelieving laugh. "That's a strange sort of question to ask."

"Not for you it isn't," the witch insisted.

The boy regarded her with an amused smile. "And why is that?"

"Because"—she lowered her voice and leaned closer—"you're something more than human."

"How did you—" The boy stopped himself from saying something he shouldn't. But he'd already given himself away, and they both knew it.

It was the witch's turn to smile. "I can hear it," she confessed. "I just don't know what it means. What you are."

Moon friends, whispered a second voice. This one was older than the first, perhaps the oldest of the voices, and she rarely made much sense.

"I'm—I'm a—" The boy stared at her, wide-eyed, curiosity and fear at war in his expression. He so clearly wanted to tell her.

But he didn't have to.

Wolf, whispered one of the seven.

At the word, the girl felt an unfamiliar hunger rip through her chest. She wanted to know everything there was to know about this wolf and his magic.

"Jack?" a woman's voice called from behind. He startled and whipped his head toward the sound.

The witch's head was suddenly a rage of noise. Seven voices repeated the name over and over in her mind, laughing and crying and shrieking, *Jack! Jack! Jack!*

"Jack," the witch whispered, and when she said his name, she felt a tendril of magic snap into place between them. But it was more than a tendril. It was a bind. And that gave her control.

Jack turned back toward the young witch, a question in his eyes. He'd felt it, too.

For a second, they stood there. A witch and a wolf bound together by the thinnest slip of magic. But it wasn't enough.

"Jack is one of your names," she said. "Give me your others."

The boy struggled against the immediate compulsion to speak, but it was no use. He was too young, and the witch was too strong. "J-J-John Cecil Callahan," he gasped.

The witch felt her power fall over him completely, felt the part of him that struggled against it. A butterfly in a net. A fish on a hook. A wolf in a trap. She could name him and, therefore, she could control him.

"Tell me what you are, Jack," the witch said.

Power, murmured the voices. *Good power.*

The boy's eyes tightened and his voice was nearly a growl when he answered, "Werewolf."

"Jack!" the woman called again, only this time, her voice was farther away. She would not be near enough to help him.

"I have to go," he said, taking a few steps. "That's my mother."

"Jack," the witch sang. "Stop right there."

The boy stopped.

"John Callahan," his mother shouted, "if you don't answer me right now!"

The boy turned pleading eyes on the young witch. He wanted to answer his mother, but some part of him already knew that the witch wouldn't allow it.

"Your will belongs to me," she whispered.

"But why?" he asked.

"Because that is the way it's supposed to be," she explained. "That is my purpose."

The boy swallowed hard and asked, "Who are you?"

The witch smiled and said, "I am nameless, but now that I have your names, you will do whatever I say."

THE WINTER PACK

Riley Callahan had waited so long to become a wolf. Now that she finally was one, she wanted to be the kind of wolf people looked up to, the kind of wolf people could trust, the kind of wolf who would never let her pack down. She wanted to be a really good werewolf.

She wasn't sure what being a wolf had to do with wearing a blindfold in the middle of the woods, but if Great Callahan said it was related, then Riley intended to do it well. She had tied her bright blue bandana firmly around her head, exactly as instructed, so that it completely covered her eyes. There would be no peeking for Riley.

"Your magic has just as much to do with being human as it does with being wolf." Riley couldn't see her mother, but she could hear her boots crunching against the frosty grass as she paced. "No matter where you are, or in what form, you must always be able to find the others of your prime."

Riley had to restrain herself from bouncing on her toes. It had been only two and a half months since she and her prime pack had been able to transform their bodies into wolves, and this was one of their first training exercises with the other young wolves. The others had all turned when they were supposed to, on the night of the first full moon of summer, and had been practicing with Great Callahan for almost nine months.

"The other four members of your prime are hidden nearby in the woods," Great Callahan explained. "They are allowed to call to you, but they are not allowed to move from their spots. Your job is to find them without transforming."

"Great Callahan?"

Riley identified the voice as that of Teddy Griffin. She pictured his sandy-brown hair and sky-blue eyes, even though they were also covered by a bandana right now.

"Yes, Teddy?"

"I don't understand why we can't transform. How are we supposed to find anything like this?" Teddy managed to sound much older than thirteen whenever he spoke, even when he was speaking to adults. Even when he was actually whining. Like now.

"You have many resources at your disposal, Mr. Griffin." Great Callahan's response was unbending. "Use them."

Riley understood Teddy's frustration. This would be much easier if she were in wolf form, when her senses were so keen she could smell another wolf a mile away. But she didn't understand questioning Mama C that way. She wasn't a regular adult. She was a great.

"Easy for you to say," Teddy grumbled.

"This is not supposed to be easy," Great Callahan continued as though she hadn't heard Teddy. And maybe she hadn't. "But the job of any alpha is to do things even if those things are difficult."

"'Do the tough stuff,'" Riley added, quoting Rule #4 of Cecelia Callahan's Alpha Code.

"That's right," Great Callahan said. "Do the tough stuff."

In total, six young wolves stood in the clearing with Great Callahan. They were all from new prime packs. All the alphas.

"Your primes are also wearing blindfolds," Great Callahan continued, her voice farther away now. "Once you have found them, your job is to lead them safely back here."

Riley thought of the other four members of her prime pack: Dhonielle Anderson, her cousin, who one hundred percent would prefer to be reading a book right now. Kenver Derry, who was probably dressed like they were going somewhere that wasn't a wintery forest. Aracely Bravo, with a heart as big as a dinosaur's. And Lydia Edgerton, who Riley was trying very hard to think of as a packmate, and not as the girl who made Riley's cheeks burn every time she smiled.

They were the Winter Pack. The five wolves who had transformed on the first full moon of winter. It had been an unconventional transformation for them, but they were different. And, in spite of all that had happened with the Devourer, Riley knew now that they were special.

"This is not a race," Great Callahan said. "This is an exercise. I want you to take your time."

"What do we get if we finish first?" called Teddy, his voice edging toward snark.

"My respect, Mr. Griffin" was Great Callahan's answer.

"Whatever that's worth," Teddy grumbled under his breath.

Riley heard it, though. And irritation sparked in her cheeks. Not only was he disrespecting their great pack leader, but he was doing the opposite of what alphas should do.

Before her first transformation, Riley had assumed that an alpha was chosen magically. That it was something decided by forces outside of a wolf's control. But the night she and her prime had transformed, there had been no magical anointing of their alpha. It had come down to the five of them. They got to choose.

We choose you, Lydia had said, speaking into Riley's mind.

And even though it was exactly what Riley wanted, some part of her worried she didn't deserve it. That she wouldn't be good at it. She asked, *Why?*

Because you worry about everything, Kenver said.

Riley hadn't understood at first. Why did worrying about everything make her a good alpha? Aracely had explained, *It's because you keep track of everything. Like a radar. You're our alpha because you notice things that matter. Like when Dhonielle is freaking out.*

I only freak out when it's called for, Dhonielle clarified. *But she's right. You're our alpha, Riley.*

Before she could stop herself, Riley said, "I'll bet I can find my prime before you do, Teddy Griffin."

Teddy snorted. "No way am I going up against you and your special treatment."

"What are you talking about?" Riley had expected a competition, not an insult. "I don't get special treatment."

"You have one hour!" called Great Callahan at that exact moment. "Except for you, Riley. You and the Winter Pack have thirty minutes."

"What were you just saying?" Teddy all but sneered.

Riley swallowed hard. This didn't feel like special treatment. This felt unfair. Not only did she have half the amount of time Teddy did to complete the same task, but he seemed to think she was getting something she most definitely was not.

"The clock starts . . . now!"

Riley heard the others begin to move. Some were going quickly, a fast walk, while others sounded as though they were shuffling forward, one small step at a time.

For the first few seconds, Riley just stood there. Her stomach pitched to one side, a sick feeling making her unsteady on her feet. She'd been caught completely off guard by Teddy's comment, and now she wondered if the others thought the same thing he did.

"Riley?" her mother asked, footsteps coming close. "Twenty-nine minutes."

Riley ground her teeth. Special treatment or not, it was a challenge, and Riley wanted to show her mom what she was capable of.

She took off at a run. Letting her feet move on instinct, just like when she was a wolf. There was no better feeling than racing as fast as she could go, her claws digging into the earth with each powerful stride, her wrists and ankles adjusting to every dip and rise of the forest floor. There was nothing like the wind singing through her teeth or the moonlight glinting between the trees.

She had none of that now, trapped in her human form, with a bandana tied around her eyes. And almost as soon as she'd started running, Riley tripped on a root and went sprawling to the ground.

Great.

She landed on her belly, with a mouthful of dirt and dead leaves. Her palms stung from the impact but at least none of the others had seen her spectacular wipeout.

"Ouch!" came another voice from somewhere to Riley's right.

"Ugh!" came another.

"Gosh darn it!" came one that could only be Erika Farrow, who said a lot of words that were almost bad without actually being bad and who wore perfume that smelled like vanilla.

It seemed that Riley's fellow alphas were faring about as well as she was.

She climbed to her feet and gently dusted off her stinging palms. Trying to move quickly was out of the question. Her sense of smell wasn't going to get her far, since the only thing she could smell was the dirt that had lodged itself up her nose. She was going to have to do this by sound.

Just as Riley opened her mouth to call to her prime, the air filled with voices. The other five alphas had come to the same conclusion and were doing exactly what she'd planned to do. They were calling to their primes. Not only that, but their primes were calling back. Twenty-five voices mingled together, creating a chaotic web of sound that was impossible to untangle. No one was going to find anyone this way. At least not in the time they'd been given.

Riley was going to have to do this another way.

Dhonielle? Riley reached out in her mind. *Lydia?* Riley

waited a beat before calling to the others. *Aracely? Kenver? Can you hear me?*

Speaking into each other's minds like this wasn't something any of the other young wolves could do. In fact, it wasn't something many other wolves could do at all. But when the Devouring Wolf had broken free of his stone prison last summer, he had ignited an old spell. One that had changed their magic and given them what they needed to defeat him.

The Devourer was gone now—back inside the stone prison, with new wards set to ensure he would never escape again—but the changes to their prime pack's magic remained.

It was Lydia who answered first. *We're here,* she assured her.

Yeah, and we're freezing our beans off, added Dhonielle. *Hurry up and find us!*

What, exactly, are your "beans"? Kenver asked.

They're . . . Nothing! It's just a thing people say, Dhonielle said quickly.

Is it, though? Kenver said.

Mmm, beans, Aracely murmured. *I really love sweet bean paste. Have you ever had it? We get it at the Asian market on Colorado Street, and it comes in these pancake things called dorayaki, and they're so delicious! But, you know, I also like kidney beans when they're in chili, and those aren't sweet at all.*

Aracely went on and on while Kenver started naming different kinds of beans, simply to see how many Aracely could talk about. Riley let their banter guide her. They weren't together—she could tell that immediately—but Kenver and Dhonielle were the closest, so Riley headed for them first.

Green beans, Kenver said.

Mm, I can't say I'm the biggest fan. Especially when they're all mushy from a can.

It was strange for Riley to move through the woods so slowly. Stranger still to feel like she knew where she was going when she couldn't see. But this was a part of wolf magic.

Most wolves developed the ability to sense the other members of their pack when they were near. The most powerful, like Great Callahan, could do it over large distances. Speaking directly into each other's minds was rare, however. So rare that Riley didn't know anyone else who could do it except the five of them.

Which was probably why Great Callahan had given her less time than all the others.

Mung beans, Kenver said.

What is a mung bean? Dhonielle asked, curiosity getting the better of her.

Oh, my aunt puts those in curry and they're so good! Aracely said.

The closer Riley came to Dhonielle's hiding place, the

easier it was to sense her. Every person in her pack felt a little different. Dhonielle felt like a vibration. Sometimes like a shiver. Sometimes like a clap of thunder. But always that sense of energy.

"You got me." Dhonielle took Riley's hand and squeezed. "Oh! You're colder than I am. C'mon, let's hurry so we can go get some hot chocolate and never do this again."

Cocoa beans! shouted Aracely.

It didn't take long after that. Riley followed the gentle, steady tug of Kenver's energy, then Aracely's, which felt like bubbles, then the warmth of Lydia's, until she had her entire prime pack at her side.

"Good work, pup. Two minutes to spare," Great Callahan said when they returned. Riley felt a rush of satisfaction.

Last summer, she'd been so afraid that she would never become a wolf. Watching the other twelve-year-olds turn into wolves at the Full Moon Rite had been one of the worst moments of her life. Everyone had looked at her and the rest of her prime like there was something wrong with them. Of course, something had been wrong, but not with them. After the Devouring Wolf broke free of his prison, he'd disguised himself as Great Callahan, stripping the wolf from several young pups.

Riley and her prime were the only ones who could fight back.

Now Riley was finally a wolf and she loved everything about it—from the ability to transform at will to the unique bond she shared with her pack. Not only that, but the rest of the wolf community was safe. Everything, every scary, terrible thing, had been worth it.

It was another fifteen minutes before anyone else returned. The first to arrive were Luke Shacklett and his prime. Even after the Devourer stole his wolf away, he'd become his prime's alpha. He gave Riley a weary nod as he tugged the bandana off his eyes, then lay on the cold ground to rest for a minute.

The remaining four primes were nearly a full fifteen minutes after that. They dragged their feet, looking cold and tired and, when they saw Riley and the others, maybe a little mad. None more so than Teddy Griffin, who glared openly.

"She cheated!" he shouted, raising a finger to point at Riley.

"What?" Riley said, anger surging. "How?"

"Don't tell lies, Teddy," Aracely added, coming to stand at Riley's shoulder.

"Teddy, I told you this wasn't a race," Great Callahan answered.

"You're only saying that because she's your daughter!" snarled Teddy. "They can do that telepathy thing, and we can't! It's not fair! It's cheating!"

Riley didn't know what to say to that. The telepathy

thing was true, but was it cheating? She could feel shame flushing hot in her cheeks, and her head felt a little dizzy.

"Every pack has different strengths," Great Callahan said evenly. "The point of this exercise is to discover yours. It has nothing to do with any other prime."

"But they can only do things like that because they're the precious 'Winter Pack.'" Teddy used air quotes to make sure everyone knew he was mocking the name.

A lump formed in Riley's throat. Teddy was right that this wasn't fair. She and the others had endured months of whispers and uncertainty, all because they hadn't transformed into wolves. She'd thought it would be better now that they could run with the rest of the pack. She'd thought everything would go back to normal.

But this wasn't normal.

Great Callahan moved between Teddy and Riley. "You accomplished something today, Teddy. You found your prime. You should spend some time thinking about that instead of this."

Teddy crossed his arms over his chest and glared at the ground, but he didn't say anything else. Behind him, the rest of his prime drew closer.

"C'mon," Teddy grumbled, leading them away.

Riley cared about only one of the members of Teddy's pack. Milo, her younger brother, trailed behind the others, his dark curls flopping into his green eyes, his body obscured inside a puffy orange parka. He hung behind just long enough to catch Riley's eye. *Sorry*, he mouthed, with a shrug, and then he was gone.

One by one, the other packs followed Teddy's. Riley tried to smile when they made eye contact, tried to be encouraging. They were all wolves, after all. All members of the same greater pack.

But no one smiled back. Instead, they drew away, their eyes suspicious and untrusting, watching the members of her prime pack, Riley thought, like they were outsiders.

2

SEEING THINGS

Winter had settled into the village of Clawroot, and every pointed rooftop glittered with frost. Dry tall grasses hissed and shivered in the chilly breeze, and garlands of snowberry vines adorned every door. Inside the buildings, cinder stones inside fireplaces glowed cherry red, providing heat without a flame, and every cabin was occupied by wolves who preferred the wild to the comforts of small-town Lawrence, Kansas.

Training was done for the day, and Great Callahan led the group of young wolves to the dining hall, which smelled like chocolate and fresh-baked cookies. Riley's mouth watered, but she stopped at the door.

"Let the others go first," she said.

"Um, whyyyyy?" When Aracely whined, her curls whined with her, drooping around her warm brown face. "All the best cookies will be gone if we wait."

"Because . . ." Riley hesitated. How was she supposed to say that she was worried the other wolves were jealous of them without seeming conceited?

"Because," Lydia chimed in, with an easy smile, "even though it wasn't a competition, we did it fastest. While we were hanging out together, most of them were still blindfolded and alone. Letting them get their hot chocolate first is the nice thing to do."

"Even if they were really sore about it," Kenver muttered, not bothering to conceal their disdain.

"That makes sense," Aracely said, though she sounded sad about it.

"Don't worry." Lydia hooked an arm through Aracely's. "Ms. Montgomery always makes plenty of cookies. But if she didn't, for some reason, I'll make you some special candy at my uncles' shop."

"You could do that anyway, you know," Aracely said, letting Lydia draw her toward the end of the cookie line.

Riley still didn't understand how Lydia always managed to find the right words, but it didn't bother her the way it used to. They were a team, a pack. And no single person in the group had to be good at everything. A pack was stronger together.

"I still can't believe Milo is in that bully's pack," Dhonielle said quietly, honeyed brown eyes locked on Teddy. "I wish there were something we could do about it. Why couldn't he have ended up with Luke? That would have been perfect for everyone."

Riley felt the same way. Her brother had just turned ten years old. He was funny and obnoxious, and more than once Riley had wanted to tell him to eat a bee, but she also cared about him, and she didn't like knowing that he was trapped in a prime pack with someone like Teddy Griffin.

But that was the thing about wolf magic. Though there were several ways to become a wolf, and even one way to *un*become one, there was no way to choose your prime. It chose you.

"Milo says he's a good alpha," Riley said, willing it to be true. "And that's the most important thing, right?"

Dhonielle made a face. "I guess. But it would be great if he wasn't also such a turd."

By the time they'd gathered steaming mugs of hot chocolate and plates piled with still-warm snickerdoodles and chocolate chip cookies, the others were already looping around for seconds.

Kenver claimed an unoccupied table at the end of the room, as far from Teddy Griffin's table as they could get. Riley had just taken her first, perfect sip of rich hot cocoa when—*Safe place . . . I need to find*—a voice landed heavily in her mind, the words at once so loud and so far away that she brought her hands to her ears and squeezed her eyes shut.

Who's there? the voice said.

It sounded like it had been fractured into a thousand pieces and glued back together again.

"Who is that?" hissed Lydia.

Riley shook her head, and when she pried her eyes open, she found that Lydia also had her hands pressed to her ears. They all did. Except for Kenver, who held a hand to their forehead as though they were in pain. Which they probably were because that voice was so—

Hello!

"I don't know, but this is super-rude," Aracely moaned.

"I didn't think anyone else could talk to us like this," muttered Dhonielle.

"I don't think they're supposed to be able to. And that's why it hur—" Kenver cut off abruptly as a vision filled each of their minds.

A girl. She was about their age, no more than thirteen or fourteen years old, with ivory skin and eyes so dark blue they were almost purple. Her hair was blond, little braids holding it back from her temples. She looked right at them, eyes wide and fearful.

Hello? Hello! Who are you?

Riley squeezed her eyes. She'd never had a vision before, and this one hurt. With one great effort, she pushed back, saying, *Stop!*

"Riley? Hey, are you okay?"

Riley blinked and found Milo standing next to her, with a look of confused concern on his face. And it wasn't just him. Everyone was looking at her, at the Winter Pack, their expressions ranging from confusion to suspicion. Luke, at least, looked worried.

It was clear to Riley that only she, Dhonielle, Lydia, Aracely, and Kenver had shared the vision of the strange girl asking for help. All the others must have seen was the five of them squinting and covering their ears, which Riley had to admit probably looked pretty weird.

Riley offered Milo a wobbly smile, determined to pretend that she and her pack were one hundred percent normal. "I'm fine," she said. "We're fine. It's just—"

"Brain burn," Aracely blurted. "It's like brain freeze, except the reverse, you know? That hot chocolate was superhot."

"O-kay . . ." Milo said slowly, looking at Aracely like he didn't believe her but he didn't know how to contradict her either. Which was one of Aracely's true gifts, Riley had learned.

As Milo left to return to his own table, Riley felt a little guilty. She didn't like lying to her brother. Or anyone. But she also didn't like the way everyone had been staring, and telling the truth wouldn't have made that part any better.

"So," Kenver said when Milo was gone, careful to keep their voice low. "We all saw that, right? Did anyone recognize their face?"

Everyone shook their heads.

"Should we tell someone?" Dhonielle asked. "Like maybe Great Callahan?"

Riley pictured the girl from the vision again. Those dark blue eyes, the fear in them. She couldn't shake the feeling that whoever the girl was, she needed help. Maybe they *should* say something.

Just then, there was a sharp spike of laughter from across the room. Riley didn't have to search long for the source. Several tables away, Teddy was holding his head and pretending to cry, in an obvious re-creation of what had just happened at her own table. And everyone around him was laughing, their gazes sliding toward the Winter Pack with glee.

Riley had assumed that becoming a wolf would fix all her problems. She'd assumed that being a wolf meant she would feel like part of the greater pack. But she'd been wrong.

If she and her prime wanted to truly be a part of the greater pack, they were going to have to stop seeming different. Strange. Special. They were going to have to fit in.

They had no idea who the girl from the vision was, and as far as Riley knew, there was no way to find out. It was like a phone call from a wrong number. Random and unimportant.

"No," Riley said definitively. "We're not going to tell anyone, because there's nothing to tell."

3

PORKENSTEIN THE PIG

Despite what she'd said, Riley spent the whole ride home still wondering if she should tell someone about the vision.

Next to her, Milo was doing his best to ignore her, which was what he'd done since Riley's first transformation.

Before the first full moon of winter, Milo had been glued to her side. So much so that it had gone from sweet to completely annoying. Every day after school, he'd brought his homework to her room and done it sitting on her floor. Then on the weekends, he'd watch TV with her in the morning, without demanding that they watch one of his shows. Without coming right out and saying anything, he'd been telling her that he loved her and was worried that she was sad because she hadn't turned into a wolf and he had.

Then Riley and the others had heard the call of First Wolf, and they'd spent a full month on the protected grounds of Wax & Wayne, learning to be wolves to-gether. They'd missed all of winter break and even two weeks of school, but that hadn't bothered any of them, because they were finally, finally wolves.

Riley had returned home expecting to find things exactly as she'd left them, and in some ways they were. The hall tree by the front door was still loaded down with purses and scarves and house keys. There were cat toys haphazardly strewn about the living room and on the stairs to the second floor. She was still expected to do all the same chores, especially cleaning out the cat litter.

But things were different, too, and they weren't easy for Riley to describe.

There was a new feeling in the house. A new wordless kind of communication, which Riley didn't remember from before. It was as if now that the whole family had transformed, they understood each other a little better. Which was good and bad. Good because it felt like a kind of magic that was unique to them, and bad because her moms were already too good at sensing when she was trying to hide something.

The biggest change had been in Milo.

He'd gone from spending too much time with her to spending next to none. In fact, he seemed to be avoid-ing her. On school nights, he stayed in his room with the door shut, from the time he got home until dinner. And on weekends, he left with his prime and returned only when he had to.

In the car now, it was no different. While Riley replayed the vision of the young girl over and over in her mind, Milo kept his eyes glued to the graphic novel in his hands. He didn't even try to make her look at the most exciting panels, which was kind of like if Aracely were to listen to music without humming along. It was too quiet. And that quiet seemed to hide something meaningful—like anger or hurt or, worse, dislike. Whatever it was, it was a wedge between the two of them.

She had already begun to worry that Teddy had something to do with it, and after today, she was nearly convinced of it.

"What are you reading?" she asked.

Milo shrugged. "Nothing you'd care about."

"How can you know unless you tell me?"

Milo sighed and shut the book to show her the cover, where a group of kids was doing battle with what looked like a giant pig. Riley had to admit that it wasn't something she'd naturally reach for, but she bobbed her head and said, "Looks cool. Is it good?"

"Yeah," Milo said, eyes brightening, as if he'd forgotten to ignore her. "I'm only halfway through, but it's really good. The bad guy's name is Porkenstein, and he's a massive pig who was struck by lightning and gained superpowers, and now he's on a quest to control all of humanity. It's not like anything I've ever read."

Riley smiled, happy that her brother was talking to her, even if it was about something she couldn't care less about.

"Teddy let me borrow it. He has an awesome collection of graphic novels, and he lets me borrow whatever I want." Milo beamed. "He's pretty great."

"Sure." Riley felt her smile deflate like a balloon. Teddy was a big part of Milo's life, which meant he was also a part of Riley's life now. Like it or not.

"Riley, when we get home, I'd like to discuss how you were able to find the Winter Pack so quickly today," Mama C called over her shoulder.

Milo rolled his eyes loudly and flipped his book open once more.

Great.

"Um, sure. I mean, I think it was pretty much the way everyone else does it," Riley said, so eager to fit in with the others that she stumbled into a lie. She hadn't meant to tell it, but there it was, dripping from her lips.

"Hmm, I'm not so sure about that," Mama C said. "But we can discuss it after dinner, okay?"

"Okay," Riley said, wishing her mom had chosen some other time to bring this up.

"Good. We need to stay on top of any changes you and the Winter Pack might be experiencing. And I need you to stay alert. Tell me if you notice anything strange or . . ."

"Special?" suggested Milo without lifing his eyes from his book. On the page, Porkenstein the Pig was standing over the kids with a maniacal grin on his pig face. A speech bubble next to him read, "You humans think you know everything, but you cannot comprehend the extent of my new powers!"

"Different," Mama C said. "Got it?"

"Yeah," Riley said softly. "I got it."

Riley was pretty sure Milo lingered on that page longer than it took for him to read it. His finger rested next to that same panel as if he wanted to make sure Riley saw it and understood that in the graphic novel of his life, she played the role of the evil pig with superpowers.

By the time they pulled into the driveway, Riley was feeling worse than ever. Milo darted out of the car and straight to his room, and Riley spent the rest of the evening trying not to draw attention to herself.

None of it was fair, but she didn't want to make it worse. And right now, it seemed like whatever she did made things worse.

4

A MYSTERY OF WITCHES

That night, Riley had hardly been asleep when something woke her. The clock on her bedside table reported that it was only ten thirty. Outside, the sky was clear, revealing a brilliant quarter moon, and the grass below glittered with frost.

Riley was trying to stay very still, listening for whatever it was that had roused her, when she heard a *thump* from downstairs and a *creeeak* just outside her door.

Moving as quietly as she could, Riley slid out of bed and crossed the room, pressing one ear against the door. *Creeeak*, she heard again, and this time she recognized the sound. Someone was in the hallway, but they weren't walking. They were sneaking.

Twisting the knob slowly, Riley eased her door open, peered into the dark hallway, and spotted a figure at the top of the stairs. They were tall and thin, with long hair tied back in a loose braid, and they were dressed in a T-shirt and sweatpants. Riley recognized them instantly.

"Darcy," Riley whispered. "What are you—"

Her sister spun around, one finger pressed to her lips indicating that Riley should be quiet. With the other hand, she beckoned Riley closer.

On tiptoes, Riley moved to the top of the stairs, next to her sister. Darcy was three and a half years older than Riley, but while Riley was broad across her shoulders like Mama C, Darcy was slight, even though the two were nearly the same height.

Downstairs, the kitchen light spilled into the living room, deepening the shadows there. She could hear voices speaking in sharp, hushed tones. It took her a moment to recognize that at least two of them didn't belong to her moms.

"Who is it?" Riley asked, in the softest whisper she could manage.

Darcy's brown eyes seemed to burn a little when she answered, "Witches."

Riley reached out to grab the banister for support. Witches? In her house? Riley knew that there were witches in Lawrence. There were witches everywhere. But to her knowledge, wolves and witches did not talk. They certainly didn't socialize late at night in her very own kitchen!

"Why are they here?" she asked, and when Darcy only shrugged, Riley made a decision that might have been considered reckless. She began to walk down the stairs.

Darcy made a soft sound of distress but didn't try to stop her as she carefully moved from one step to the next. Riley held her breath, as though that would have any impact on whether a stair squeaked or not. Still, it made her feel better, so she didn't breathe until she was only four steps from the bottom. Close enough to hear what was being said inside the kitchen.

"I understand that this comes as a shock," said a voice Riley didn't recognize.

"That is an understatement, Ms. Mercy." That had come from Mama C. And she did not sound pleased.

"We're not happy about it either, but there is nothing we can do. What's done is done. We offer this talisman in the spirit of peace and making amends."

"I'm sure my uncle will be very happy that his bones are being offered to make amends."

"Cecelia," Mama N said in her soothing way.

"Don't, Nina," Mama C snapped. Riley couldn't remember hearing Mama C ever talk to Mama N like that before. "There are decades of bad blood here. The Free Witches are responsible for the gruesome death of my uncle, among others."

Riley's head spun. She knew that Mama C didn't trust witches and that it was because of something that had happened in the past, but she'd never heard the whole story.

"Look, I get that you're mad," said a new voice. "But

you need to remember that we didn't have to bring you that talisman. Heck, we didn't have to come at all, but we're here because our coven was a part of this problem and now we'd like to help fix it."

"Your coven is responsible for the single greatest terror in all of wolf history." Mama C sounded closer now. Like she'd come perilously near to the door. One more step and she'd see her daughter hiding in the stairway.

Riley's heart was pounding in her ears. She pressed her back to the wall and concentrated on not making a sound.

"You'll have to excuse me if I'm not sympathetic to your desire for amends. Now please see yourselves out."

"All right. We understand," Ms. Mercy said firmly. "Please just think about what we said. She's out there, and we don't know where. So if you need us, for any reason, you only need to call. Ms. Books knows where to find us, I believe."

"That is her job." Mama C didn't sound angry anymore, but she sounded dangerous in a way Riley wasn't used to.

She froze. And it was at that exact moment that the two witches left the kitchen and walked right past the stairs, where Riley was hiding in plain sight.

One of them turned, her eyes traveling up and locking on Riley. The witch's face was cast in shadow. All Riley could see was the twinkle of light in her eyes as she spotted her and the rainbow cardigan that draped around her soft hips. Riley thought she saw the witch begin to smile, but then she was gone, headed toward the front door with her friend.

Heart hammering, Riley spun on her heel and climbed the stairs as quietly as she could manage, nearly crashing into Darcy at the top. Together, they hurried down the hallway toward their separate bedrooms.

Just before Riley shut her door, she saw Milo peering through a crack in his own door across the hall.

"What happened?" he whispered.

Riley considered for just a second before answering. "Nothing," she said. Then she shut the door and dove into bed.

Very little she'd heard tonight made much sense, but one thing was clear: the witches were worried about something, or someone, and it was bad enough that they'd come to warn the wolves.

5

THE TALISMAN

The next day, their usual training session was canceled. Instead, everyone was directed to the amphitheater for an emergency forum.

"What's an 'emergency forum'?" Aracely asked, looking expectantly at Riley.

"It means that something has happened that the pack needs to know about." Riley hadn't had a chance to tell her prime about the witches in her house last night. Then again, she wasn't sure what she could say about them. She'd heard only half of a conversation. She had more questions about it than answers.

"It's probably bad news," Dhonielle said, lips twisting into a pout. "These kinds of things are always bad news."

"Then we'd better not be the last to hear it." Lydia ushered them after the other primes, already transforming for the journey.

They were gathered in the parking lot of Wax & Wayne, the same place they always gathered before heading to the amphitheater, and while they could easily make the short trip in human form, there was no reason not to go as wolves.

Riley didn't think she would ever get tired of shifting into wolf form.

She loved the way magic felt in her body, the way it fizzed up through her skin like she was a can of soda ready to burst. She leapt, and the transformation flooded through her, tugging at her teeth and claws and toes, until she was a wolf, her fur so dark gray it was almost black. Shadowy and perfect.

All around her, the rest of her pack shivered and shook into wolf form, and Riley drank in the sight of them. Aracely was earthy brown, with drops of honey sprinkled throughout like freckles, including one fleck at the very tip of her tail. It caught the light like one of her lithocharms, guiding them through the woods. Kenver was sleek and silver. They looked like a streak of starlight through the underbrush. Lydia was a creamy color, with snow white highlighting her ears and tail. And Dhonielle was a deep red, with even darker stripes running the length of her body.

They raced through the winter woods, leaves crunching beneath their paws, twigs and old vines snapping around their bodies. Their breath fogged hot before their faces as the cold wind raked through their fur.

One of the best parts about being a wolf was that

they could travel so much faster than they could in their human bodies, and the two miles of woods passed in a matter of moments. Almost before any of them had noticed, they'd rushed past the familiar cabins that housed them during Tenderfoot Camp and arrived at their destination. They took a moment to shift back into their human forms before heading into the amphitheater.

There was already a crowd gathering. The rows of benches ringed around a massive firepit at the center were almost full already. There were dozens upon dozens of people, and Riley marveled that they'd all managed to get here so quickly.

The amphitheater was packed, and Riley wasn't sure where to go until she spotted Darcy seated with her prime on a bench in the last row. Riley made a beeline for them, reaching back to catch Dhonielle's hand and keep her own prime together.

"Lilee!" called Darcy, waving her over.

"Hey, Winter Pack." This came from Darcy's alpha, Evan Westfall. "Here. We'll stand. You guys hop up."

Without an ounce of hesitation, the rest of Darcy's prime stood up and offered their bench to the younger wolves, letting them climb atop the bench so they could see what was about to happen below.

"Do you think this is about . . . ?" Riley said to her sister.

"Maybe," Darcy answered. "Probably."

Just then, Great Callahan stepped into the center of the amphitheater. She was dressed warmly, in a navy-blue wool coat that hung to her knees and slouchy black boots. Hanging around her neck was a chunk of pale rock wrapped in a thick band of silver. It swung over her chest on a long leather cord. It was notable because her mother didn't wear much jewelry, other than her wolf cuff, and Riley had never seen her wear it before.

Next to Great Callahan were the other two greats of the Hackberry Hill Alliance: Great Mort and Great Williams. The first was a tall, tree of a man, with a puff of white hair atop his head like a cloud. The latter was a lean old woman, with short hair dyed in spikes of black and fuchsia in addition to her natural silver.

"Thank you for gathering so quickly," Great Callahan said, and a hush immediately settled over the crowd. "First, I want to assure you that what I am about to tell you is all we know. We will be monitoring the situation closely, but as of now, we are asking that no immediate actions be taken. Any actions taken by individuals or primes will not be supported by the Hackberry Hill Alliance."

In the pause that followed, no one made a sound.

"We've just received word that the Nameless Witch will soon die, and a successor has been chosen to take her place."

Riley didn't hear whatever her mother said next. Not

only because her mind was racing, but because Aracely's mind was, too. Riley could hear Aracely's voice in her head saying, *Whaaaaawhawhawhawhawhaaaaaaaaaaaat?*

Dhonielle clapped a hand over Aracely's mouth and, in spite of the fact that it was her brain and not her mouth making the sound, the noise stopped.

"The Nameless Witch?" Riley aimed the question down at her sister, who was standing just below Riley, on the ground.

Darcy nodded distantly, eyes still locked on their mother.

"This would be reason enough for concern," Great Callahan was saying, "but we've also learned that her successor is here in Kansas. Not in Lawrence, but somewhere in one of the western covens. And she's missing."

A murmur rippled through the crowd.

Riley had so many questions, but most of them were answered by the expression she saw on the faces around her. Everyone knew that the Nameless Witch was real. That was why her story was so terrifying. Because it had actually happened. But when the young wolves told the story around campfires or late at night when the adults were asleep, they told it because some part of them didn't believe it could happen to them.

Now, though, Riley saw that every adult around her was worried. Scared. And even though Riley didn't fully understand why, she felt their fear like an echo in her own lungs, making it a little harder to draw a full breath.

"The spell has been initiated, and it will go into full effect on the spring equinox," Great Williams called in her reedy, thin voice. "That's two weeks until she's a real threat to anyone."

Great Mort raised his hands and spoke in a booming voice, "Our relationship with the Free Witches of Lawrence remains respectful, and we don't anticipate any issues, but this is a matter of great concern. It is also, potentially, an opportunity."

Riley didn't have time to wonder what he meant, because Great Callahan spoke again.

"The witches want us to help recover the next Nameless Witch so that they can keep her locked up, as they always have," she said. "But handing her over would be like handing a weapon to our greatest enemy. If we can find and capture the witch, we can end her reign of terror. So we are asking everyone to stay cautious and let us know if you encounter anything of note."

At that, the crowd began to disperse, everyone muttering quietly to their neighbors as they filed out of the rows.

"Darcy!" Riley grabbed the sleeve of her sister's knee-length pea jacket and tugged. "What is going on?"

"I think Mom just explained it," she said gently.

"Okay." Riley released her sister and held up a finger. "But what does it mean that a *new* Nameless Witch is being chosen or whatever? And why does witch stuff matter to us?"

"Witch stuff always matters to us," Darcy explained. "Just . . . sometimes it matters more than others. Like now."

"Why?" Dhonielle asked.

"Because . . ." Darcy took a deep breath, then puffed it out. "A long time ago, one of the Free Witches was chosen as the Nameless Witch. Before her, wolves didn't really care about the Nameless Witch, because she didn't have much to do with us. But the Free Witch? She was different. She was the one we tell stories about. The one we sing that song about. She was the one who killed wolves."

Riley gasped. She knew those stories well. The Nameless Witch had stolen things from wolves. Power, mostly, but also parts of their bodies—like claws and teeth and even paws. And she'd turned them into talismans . . .

Riley's eyes widened at her realization. She searched for Mama C and spotted her standing at the nearest exit, pausing to reassure Aracely's parents. And there, hanging on her chest, was the strange stone necklace Riley had noticed earlier. Except it wasn't a stone, she now knew. It was bone.

"Our uncle?" Riley asked, stunned by the gruesomeness.

Darcy nodded solemnly.

"It hasn't been a problem for a long time, because after that, they started locking up the Nameless Witches," Darcy explained. "But if the new one is missing, then who knows what will happen."

"Just remember," Evan said, leaning toward Riley as though he were imparting wisdom, alpha to alpha. "Never trust a witch, and never give them your name."

IF YOU GIVE A WITCH YOUR NAME . . .

If you give a witch your name
You know just what she'll do
Once she knows the words to use
She'll put a spell on you
She'll sing a song and make demands
Double dee, hubble dee, bubble dee, bell
You'll follow each of her dark commands
That's the way of a witch's spell

6

THE GIRL IN THE WOODS

Riley awoke with a start. She was surprised to find that she was standing up and not in her bed, as she'd expected to be, but even more surprising was the fact that she was in the woods. The night was thick around her, the sky above glittering between bare winter branches.

"Not again," Riley mumbled, spinning around to try and get her bearings.

The last time this had happened, it had been the Devouring Wolf's magic that drew Riley and the others into the dark woods of Wax & Wayne. It had been terrifying and confusing, but at least it hadn't been freezing. She bounced from one foot to the next as her bare feet burned with cold. Why did this always have to happen in the middle of the night? When she was barefoot and in her pajamas? At least this time, she had a few advantages. The first was that she knew her prime must also be out here somewhere and that she could find them. The second was that she wasn't the same wolfless girl she'd been last summer.

Riley drew on the wolf inside her, letting her shape shift from that of a lanky thirteen-year-old with dark brown hair and wintery-pale skin, to that of a wolf with a thick coat of fur and paws that were tougher than feet. Instantly, she felt warmer—and safer, too. She tipped her face up, toward the sky, and let out a crystal-clear wolf call.

It was only a second before she heard an answering call. Then another, and another, and another, as Kenver and Aracely and Lydia and Dhonielle sounded off.

Riley wanted to run to them, but she held still and howled again, holding the note for as long as possible. After a few more seconds, her prime appeared one by one, until all five of them were standing together.

Really could have done without this ever happening again, Kenver said, voice groggy and grumpy.

I'm going to start sleeping with shoes on, Aracely whined. *And my toes really need to breathe at night.*

Toes . . . don't . . . breathe? Dhonielle said, a question in her voice, and even though she was in her wolf body, there was a clear frown on her furry face.

My *toes do*, Aracely answered.

Any ideas on what brought us here? Lydia had directed her question to Riley.

Riley shook her head back and forth. *But if it's*

anything like last time, it won't be long before we—

Wait! Aracely cut in. *I smell something. And before any of you say it, no, it's not* me.

Dhonielle laughed, and Lydia said, *I smell it, too. It's—*

Human? Kenver said. *But that's not supposed to be possible. There are look-aways around the perimeter that make humans, well, look away and then walk away. They aren't supposed to be able to make it this far inside Wax & Wayne.*

Riley sniffed the air and caught the unmistakable scent of a person—salty and a little stinky and a little sweet. Bodies made all kinds of odors. That was something she'd had to get used to very quickly as a young wolf. Her sense of smell was keen even in her human form, and that hadn't always been a good thing. Especially at school. It took some kids way too long to realize they could stink just like everyone else.

Mama N had told Riley that bodies create smells for a reason and they were just a part of life. They stank when they needed to be cleaned, were sour when they were expelling toxins, and were earthy or sweet when they were happy.

"As a wolf, it will be important for you to learn how bodies smell," Mama N had told her after Riley had come home from school complaining about how one of her classmates reeked terribly of blood and baby powder. "And as a human, it's important for you to remember that you are also going through a lot of changes right now and doing your best. Let everyone else do their best, too."

Riley still thought her classmates smelled, but she'd gotten better at recognizing certain scents. Like sour breath or freshly washed hair, or menstruation. None of them were bad, but they all meant different things.

This person in the woods smelled sharp. Salt and copper and heat. It set Riley's nerves on edge.

Go slowly, she warned, creeping along in near silence.

She could sense the person a few yards ahead. Crouched behind the trunk of a great big sycamore, they shivered quietly. Riley heard the rasp of their breath and the very faint chatter of their teeth.

They were freezing and they were afraid, but were they also dangerous?

Mama C said it didn't take much to make a person dangerous. Fear and desperation could push even the gentlest of souls toward violence, but this person was hiding. They'd also, as Kenver pointed out, somehow made it past the look-aways and wards, which suggested maybe they weren't totally human after all.

Riley hesitated. She was curious and wanted to help, but a good alpha also had to take care of their own pack. She needed to be careful now and not put them in danger.

Stay hidden, she told the others, and then she nosed forward, circling around the big tree and pushing through the tangle of winter vines until she saw her.

A girl huddled into a ball, with her knees tucked up beneath a dark purple coat and a hood pulled over her hair. The toes of black boots peeked out from the bottom of her coat, and she clutched a brown leather backpack to her chest. She had white skin, her cheeks bright pink with the cold, and when Riley looked into her face, she was shocked to find that the girl's dark blue eyes were trained on her. Not only that, but Riley recognized this girl.

She stepped back in shock.

It was the girl from the vision.

7

DEFINE "MOSTLY"

The girl froze, but she didn't scream, and her eyes didn't widen with fear, which would be a normal reaction to seeing a wolf standing not six feet away from you in the woods. Instead, the girl seemed to relax a little. A small sigh escaped her lips.

A moment ago, this girl had clearly been terrified. Now, she wasn't.

And that made Riley nervous.

Seeming to sense the wolf's unease, the girl held up her hands, palms out, as if in surrender, and slowly rose to her feet. Now Riley could see that the girl was about her age, and that her coat was a short cloak that swirled around her thighs. She wore distressed black jeans, tucked into boots with crisscrossed purple laces. She was dirty. And now that Riley was closer, she could identify the smells: sweat—days of it; gasoline; and just the faintest hint of honeysuckle.

"Hello," the girl said.

It's her! squeaked Dhonielle. *The girl from our vision!*

What should we do? Aracely asked.

Stay back, Riley commanded, though she took another cautious step forward.

"You're the wolf I saw in my mind," the girl said. Her eyes skipped over to the others, landing on each of them briefly. "I saw all of you. Oh, I knew it. I *knew* I would find you if I just came here."

The girl's lips trembled slightly, and Riley thought she could see tears brimming in her eyes. Still, Riley waited.

"I—I know I'm not supposed to be here," the girl continued. "But I didn't know where else to go." She brought a hand to her head and paused for a few seconds. "I'm sorry. I should introduce myself." She took a deep breath before adding, "My name is Teralyn Grimsley of the Flint Witch Coven."

She's a witch! cried Aracely. She rushed forward at the same time, straight into the clearing.

Teralyn startled back, hands raised in front. "Whoa, whoa. I'm not here to hurt you. I promise. And, I mean, I know you don't have any reason to believe me, but I'm telling the truth."

Well, now we know she's lying, Aracely muttered.

She's the witch, Kenver said. *The one everyone's looking for.*

The next Nameless Witch? Dhonielle sounded frightened

now, and Riley didn't blame her. *Why do you think that?*

She got past the wards without setting them off, Kenver reasoned. *Who could do that except a powerful witch?*

That much was true. If the wards had been breached, and if anyone knew about the wards being breached, these woods would be filled with wolves looking for the culprit. As far as Riley could tell, it was only her prime pack out here.

If she's the *witch, shouldn't we, I don't know, get out of here?* Dhonielle's voice trembled at the end of her question.

Riley understood her cousin's fear, but the magic had brought them here for a reason.

I don't think so, Riley said. *At least, not until we talk to her.*

Drawing on the magic that lived in her chest, Riley let the transformation move through her. She'd never done this in front of anyone who wasn't a wolf before, and every instinct inside her demanded that she stop. But this girl already knew what they were, so there was no point in hiding it.

Riley imagined her magic like the petals of a flower, furling and unfurling between her two selves, wolf and girl, animal and human, until she was standing before the witch in nothing but one of Darcy's hand-me-down David Bowie Henleys and a pair of gray sweatpants.

Teralyn's mouth dropped into a little O of surprise. Then she smiled hopefully.

"H-hi," Teralyn said. "Wow, that was . . . That was beautiful. You're beautiful."

Riley had no idea what to say to that, but she could feel her cheeks flushing from something other than the cold.

"And that was something I should have kept to myself." Teralyn smiled. "I'm so sorry. I'm always doing that. It's just, I think magic is so stunning, and I've never seen any kind of wolf magic. I—" She stopped herself, then cleared her throat. "You can call me Ter, but before you say anything, you should remember to never tell me your name."

Evan Westfall's warning from the evening before rang in Riley's mind: *Never trust a witch, and never give them your name.*

"I wasn't going to," Riley said

"Oh." Ter looked momentarily surprised. Then she nodded. "Okay. Good."

"What are you doing here?" Riley did her best to sound as authoritative as Mama C.

"I, um, well, I need your help." Ter twisted her hands together nervously.

"Our help?" Riley said. "But we're wolves. Witches don't come to wolves for help."

"That's true. Or it's usually true. But I think you're the only ones who can help me. I think that's why I saw you in my vision. I was looking for anyone who could help me, and . . ." She took a deep breath. "Let me start at the beginning. Okay?"

Riley was starting to feel suspicious again, but she nodded.

Ter licked her lips nervously and continued. "Three days ago, I was just an ordinary witch. I wasn't anyone special or notable even. Just a girl from middle-of-nowhere Kansas, dreaming of the day I would be old enough to finally go somewhere else." She smiled apologetically. "Not that I don't love Kansas. I do. But my family is . . . Well, let's just say I've always been something of a misfit."

"What does that have to do with you being here?" Riley asked. The cold was seeping in again, and her toes were starting to go numb.

"Just that three days ago, I was normal. Then there was a big spell. And now . . ." Ter hesitated, her eyes moving from Riley to Aracely, who was giving her a more menacing wolf-stare. "Now I'm the next Nameless Witch."

Riley's mind filled with voices, all clamoring at once.

Stop! shouted Riley.

For a brief second, there was silence. Then it all started up again.

We should take her to the greats, Lydia insisted.

Quick, Kenver! How do we stun a witch? Aracely asked.

This isn't Star Trek, Dhonielle answered.

We don't have to stun her, Kenver answered. *We just have to convince her to come with us.*

Out loud, Riley repeated her earlier question, "But what are you doing here?"

"I'm here because," Ter began, drawing a deep breath, "I don't *want* to be the next Nameless Witch. I'm here because when the spell chose me, I ran away. I ran, and they chased me. And I needed somewhere to go, so I did a seeking spell. I asked the magic to show me someone who could help me, and it showed me you." Ter clasped her hands in front of her. "I need your help."

"How do you think we can help you?" Riley asked.

"There is a coven here called the Free Witches of Lawrence. They're not as traditional as the Flint Witches, and I think they might be willing to help me sever the spell before it takes hold."

That was the third time Riley had heard about the Free Witches in the last two days. First in her own kitchen and then again from Darcy at the emergency forum.

"Why do you need help for that?" Riley asked.

"Because the person my coven sent after me beat me here. I think he knew where I was headed and"—she grimaced a little—"he's a hunter."

"You led a hunter here?" Riley asked, teeth bared. Next to her, Aracely growled.

"No, no, no. I lost him," Ter said quickly. "But I thought what better place to hide from a hunter than behind wolf wards?"

She's not wrong, Kenver said. *And that's actually really smart. I have to respect smart.*

"I just need a place to hide for a few days while I figure out how to contact the Free Witches without the hunter noticing. That's the part I need your help with," Ter explained. "After that, I'll go. And with any luck, you'll never hear about me or any Nameless Witch again."

"You're saying that you can break the spell?" Riley asked. "The Nameless Witch would just end?"

Ter nodded. "That's what I'm saying."

The woods grew very silent but for the occasional squeak and creak of branches in the breeze. In spite of it being almost spring, there was a hint of snow in the air, and Riley thought there might be literal chunks of ice forming in her bloodstream.

We can't trust her, Dhonielle said quietly. *Can we?*

I still think we should take her to the greats, Lydia said. *Let them figure this out.*

But what about the vision? Kenver asked. *We saw her; she saw us. It has to mean something.*

I wish magic came with a manual. Why does it always have to be so mysterious? Aracely complained.

Riley didn't disagree with any of them. This felt too big, too important, for five thirteen-year-olds to deal with. Especially when Mama C had expressly said to report anything unusual.

She'd also said that capturing the witch would give

them an opportunity to change things. When she'd said it, Riley hadn't given much thought to how her mom would end the Nameless Witch. She hadn't given much thought to who the Nameless Witch might be. Now that she'd met Ter, there was something about her mother's words that felt threatening. What would Mama C and the greats do to Ter if they found her?

Their magic had brought them here. Magic had brought Ter to them for help. And even though Riley had been told all her life not to trust witches, she was supposed to trust her magic.

Ter said she didn't want to become the Nameless Witch, and if it was true, it was a good thing. It would certainly be good for wolves.

"Why should we trust you?" Riley asked.

Ter bit down on one side of her lower lip as she thought. "I stopped you from giving me your name," she said at last.

It was a small thing, but it had been honest.

"And why don't you want to be the Nameless Witch?" Riley asked.

"Because the Nameless Witch spends her life trapped in a bespelled room that she can never escape. Because she is hardly more than a vessel for magic for other people." Ter put her hands on her hips and lifted her chin defiantly. "And because no one asked me first and that's not fair."

Riley knew how that felt. They all did. No one had asked them last summer if they wanted to be the only five wolves capable of standing up to the Devouring Wolf. It had just happened. It had been scary and isolating and so unfair.

You're about to agree to help her, aren't you? Lydia asked.

I think we should, Riley answered.

I wouldn't want to live my life in a magic prison, Aracely mourned. *Especially if I hadn't done anything to deserve it. I mean, if I'd killed someone or something, well, I probably wouldn't do that, but if I* had *then I still wouldn't want to spend the rest of my life in a prison, but at least then I would deserve it.*

If we help her, we could help end the Nameless Witch, Riley said.

This seems like a mostly bad idea, Dhonielle mused.

Define "mostly," Kenver challenged.

At least sixty percent.

Riley nodded and said, *But if it works, it will be one hundred percent good.*

"Okay," Riley announced. "You can stay here for three days. Just until we help you find the Free Witches."

Ter nearly melted in relief. "Thank you! Thank you so much!"

8

THE YIPPERY

What should we do with her? Lydia asked.

We need a good hiding place. Somewhere no one will think to look. Dhonielle settled down on her haunches as she thought. Somehow, even in her wolf form, she managed to look like a skittish little bird with great big eyes.

Do you think all witches smell this good? Aracely inched forward, sniffing at the end of Ter's purple cloak. She sneezed and nearly fell over.

Ter laughed kindly and reached out a hand for Aracely to smell. "Hello, pretty wolf. Your coat is speckled with little stars. Can I call you Freckles?"

Aracely gave a small yip. *I like that.*

"Nice to meet you, Freckles," Ter said. Even though she couldn't hear Aracely, her approval was obvious.

We should all have fake names for her to use, Aracely continued in Riley's mind. *We can call Riley Alpha—that'll be easy. I'm Freckles because the witch says so. Dhonielle can be Kitty because she's always the scaredy cat. Kenver can be—*

Kay, Kenver interjected. *Just Kay.*

And Lydia can be Blondie because of her hair. There. Fake names for everyone. Aracely huffed, her wolf shoulders deflating a bit. *Oh no, this is going to be really hard. How am I going to remember all of these and when to use them?*

Once we get her hidden, you won't have to worry about it that much, Riley assured her. *We just need a good spot.*

Easier said than done, Kenver grumbled. *Every wolf and witch for miles is looking for her.*

"We're trying to figure out where to hide you," Riley explained. "The pack already knows that you're missing and are on the lookout, so we need to be careful. We can't just hide you in one of our closets."

"I'd rather stay behind the wards anyway."

"Because of the hunter." Riley had almost forgotten that in addition to being on the run from a terrible fate, Ter was being pursued by a hunter. It was so overwhelming that Riley wanted to apologize even though she had nothing to do with it.

Except she clearly had *something* to do with it or she wouldn't have woken up in the middle of the woods with her prime pack.

How about the Tenderfoot Camp cabins? Dhonielle suggested. *It's still behind the wards, she'd have shelter, and no one goes there this time of year.*

That's a great idea, Lydia echoed. *It'll be easier to hide her scent if she's indoors, too.*

"We have a plan. There are some cabins that don't get used until summer where you can stay," Riley said with a smile, then hesitated, realizing that they were on the far western edge of Wax & Wayne. "But they're kind of far from here."

"It's okay. I can fly," Ter said.

Witches can actually *fly?!* Aracely asked, echoing Riley's own surprise.

"Do you . . . need a broom or something?" Riley asked.

Ter laughed again, her voice light in spite of her current circumstances. "I haven't needed a broom since I turned eleven."

"Oh," Riley answered, not understanding, but Ter explained, "It's like training wheels for witches."

"Then let's go," Riley said, already transforming back into her wolf shape as the others darted ahead.

Ter, true to her word, shoved at the ground with her boots, sending her body several feet into the air, then she was flying after the wolves, keeping pace with them as they wove through the trees.

Riley followed just behind, unable to look away from the sight of a girl in a purple cloak zipping through the woods.

Moments later, they spilled onto the grounds of Tenderfoot Camp.

The cabins stood in a ring around a chaotic cluster of picnic tables and empty stands where garbage cans would be in the summertime. For two months out of the year, this place was buzzing with activity, but for the rest of the year it was abandoned. Riley had spent three summers here and every time she'd ended up in a cabin named The Yippery.

As camp cabins went, it wasn't all that special except for the fact that it was the perfect distance from the bathhouse, not too far and not too close. Other than that, it matched all the others. It had four windows and three sets of bunk beds inside. It had a green tin rooftop and a narrow porch with five steps. And on the inside of the front door was a deep gouge where, legend had it, someone had tried and failed to charge a phone battery using lithomancy and the battery exploded.

It would be strange to put Ter in any of the other cabins, so Riley led them to the Yippery, where one by one, each of the others shifted back into their human forms.

Lydia went first, then Kenver and Aracely, with Dhonielle hard on their heels. The transformation riffled through their bodies like a shimmering heat, wolf bodies fading into human.

"Oh." Ter brought her hands to her mouth in wonder. "I'm sorry, I just—I think magic is so beautiful."

Riley was amazed that someone in Ter's situation could find anything beautiful. She was on the run, being pursued by a hunter, not to mention every wolf and witch around, and she was smiling. It made Riley want to protect her and she hardly knew the girl.

"Let's get inside," Riley said, gesturing to Dhonielle, who hurried forward and, cupping her hands around the doorknob, howled quietly to pick the lock.

The door swung open, and they piled inside the empty cabin.

"Teeth and claws, it's cold in here," Aracely said, opening her mouth to watch her breath puff out in front of her. "I didn't think it was possible for it to feel colder inside than out. Someone turn on the heat."

The cabin looked lifeless without colorful sleeping bags draped over every bunk bed or large duffels spilling clothing onto the floor.

"No one uses these in the winter," Kenver reminded them. "There's no firestone to activate."

"Oof," Aracely said with a shudder. "I'm glad I'm not staying here. I would freeze my little beans off."

"Ha. Ha," Dhonielle said. "Beans for brains."

"It's okay," Ter said, smiling at their banter. "I'll be fine."

"You probably got this already, but I'm Freckles." Aracely dotted her finger across her nose to illustrate. "And, um, please don't talk to me too much because I'm really afraid I'll accidentally tell you my or someone's name and then who knows what would happen but probably something bad and—"

Dhonielle put a hand on Aracely's arm, quieting her panicked rant. "You can call me Kitty. My pronouns are she/her. So are hers," she said jabbing a thumb at Aracely. "It's nice to meet you."

"Nice to meet you, Kitty," Ter said politely.

"Kay," Kenver said with a wave. "They/them."

"You can call me Blondie," Lydia said with a wry smile for Aracely. "Apparently. And she/her."

"It's fitting," Ter said, admiring Lydia's blond curls even though they were messy at the moment. "And my pronouns are she/her or they/them."

A howl sounded in the distance. They all quieted down to listen, their hearts jumping to full speed.

"Just a coyote," Dhonielle said with relief.

"Still, we should go," Lydia said. "If one of my uncles wakes up in the middle of the night and I'm gone, I won't be able to leave the house until I turn sixteen."

"Go," Ter said, ushering them toward the door.

"You'll be safe here," Riley told her.

"You probably shouldn't turn on the lights," Kenver warned. "Just in case."

"Right, and tomorrow I'll bring you some blankets and food," Riley offered.

"I have a little bit of food left and my clothes are warmer than they look," Ter promised. "I don't need much. Just a place to hide. And thanks to you, I have that."

The others filed out of the cabin ahead of Riley, already transforming for the journey home. Riley paused and turned back to face Ter. She had so many more questions to ask, but mostly, she was struck by the fact that Ter was still smiling. She wasn't angry or shouting or crying or anything. She was dealing with horrible things, but she wasn't being horrible herself.

Riley wanted to tell her it would be okay, but she couldn't make that promise. So instead, she mirrored Ter's smile and simply said, "Good night, Ter."

"Good night," Ter said back.

9

THE TALK

The house was dark when Riley loped down the driveway, but for the single light glowing by the front door.

She stopped in the shelter of the trees, trying to decide how she should get back inside. If she'd been planning to sneak out in the middle of the night, or if she'd even been conscious for it, she could have planned for this moment. Instead, she was stuck wondering if the magic that had whisked her away to the woods had thought to leave a door unlocked. And if so, which one. The front or the back?

Realizing that she was going to have to check both doors, Riley shifted into her human form and hurried toward the front steps. The door was locked, so she hurried around the side of the house, unlatched the side gate as quietly as she could, then crossed the patio to the sliding glass door.

Holding her breath and mentally crossing her fingers,

Riley tugged at the heavy door. At first, nothing hap-pened. Then it slid open. Riley nearly collapsed into the kitchen in relief. She was inside, where it was warm, and her bed was so close. If she was lucky, no one would ever know she'd been missing.

She had just closed the door and locked it when the light snapped on.

Riley squinted at the sudden brightness and held up a hand to shield her eyes.

"Do you know what time it is?" Mama C asked.

"I—" Riley floundered, wishing she could give her mom an answer that didn't make her sound so guilty. "No," she admitted.

"It's after three." Mama C paused. "In the morning."

Riley dared a look at her mother, eyes still watering from the light.

"And where is your phone?"

Riley's shoulders slumped. She didn't have it. Or, more accurately, the superamazing magic that had trans-ported her to the woods had failed to consider equipping her with useful things like shoes or phones or permission.

"In my room." It was a guess, but since it was the last place she'd seen her phone, it seemed like a good one.

Just then, Riley's gaze caught on a mop of curly dark hair. Green eyes peeked around the doorjamb. Milo.

She glared, hoping he would leave, but he stayed put. Watching—and hearing—everything.

Mama C shook her head in disappointment. "Are you going to tell me what you were doing?"

The truth bolted through Riley's mind. Along with the almost overwhelming urge to tell her mother everything. But part of her hesitated. The last time something this important had happened in Riley's life, her mother hadn't been her mother at all, but the Devourer in disguise. She knew that wasn't the case right now. She knew it. But Riley couldn't shake the feeling that she needed to be careful about what she said to Mama C.

"Well?" Mama C crossed her arms, and Riley's eyes caught on the talisman the witches had given her.

Had they been Free Witches? Right here in this very kitchen just one night earlier? And what was it they'd said? *Ms. Books knows how to find us?* It was exactly what Ter had asked for, and if helping Ter find the Free Witches could mean no more Nameless Witch, then Riley could keep a secret for three days. Besides, Mama C herself had said they needed to find the Nameless Witch, to end her reign of terror. Riley was just going about it in a different way. Mama C might be upset when she found out, but maybe she would understand, too.

Riley was doing what was best for wolves. But she was also doing what was best for herself. Ter wasn't just some faceless witch anymore. She was a real person. A person who wore a purple cloak and smiled even when she was scared. She was someone Riley would remember forever if something bad were to happen to her.

"I was . . ." She hesitated, searching for something that was at least a little bit true.

"Out with your prime?" offered Mama C. "Or at least one member of your prime?"

"Yes," Riley admitted. "I was. I'm sorry."

"Riley, you can't run off like that. Especially so late at night. Especially right now. Do you understand what's out there? Do you understand what could happen to you?" Mama C reached up to clasp the bone talisman hanging around her neck. "You have to be more careful. Please, I need you to be more careful. Okay?"

Riley wished she could tell her mom that they didn't need to be afraid of the next Nameless Witch, but instead she only nodded.

Mama C reached out with her warm hands and tugged Riley close. "Teeth and claws! You're frozen solid. We'll discuss consequences in the morning, but for now, go to bed. Get some sleep."

"Okay." Riley smiled in relief, eager to get into her very warm, very soft bed. Thinking about this tomorrow morning was a great idea.

She was just about to head up the stairs when her mom called, "And Riley? I don't expect to have this conversation again. Understand?"

"I understand," said Riley. The real question, though, was: Did the magic understand?

• • •

Riley woke up in her own bed Sunday morning, with sunlight streaming through her window. There were two cats pinning her legs beneath a quilt, she could smell bacon cooking, and she had to pee like never before, but first she reached for her phone and fired off a text to her prime.

Everyone good?

Seconds later, a flurry of texts arrived assuring her that everyone else had made it home without incident. She was the only one who'd been caught. That, at least, was a relief. It meant no other concerned parents would be calling hers to report group delinquency.

Riley sent another text: **I think Bethany Books knows how to find what we need, but there's no way my moms are going to let me leave today.**

It was Lydia who responded: **Great! We have time. Let's talk to her after school tomorrow.**

Unable to hold it any longer, Riley scrambled down the hallway and had just finished in the bathroom when Mama N appeared out of nowhere.

"Good morning," she sang. "Or I guess it's afternoon now. Before you do anything today, your job is to scrub that bathroom from head to toe."

Riley slumped, but she accepted her punishment without protest. She knew from experience that protest would only mean more punishment.

Exchanging her pajamas for an old T-shirt and a ratty pair of shorts, Riley sprayed and scrubbed until the bathroom glinted. If she wanted to be released from extra chores anytime before the next century, she knew her work needed to be impressive. Flawless. So she scrubbed everything again just to be sure.

By the time she was done, the sun was setting on a day that had been far too short and far too empty of searching for Free Witches.

Mama C was waiting for Riley when she returned to her bedroom.

"How are you feeling?" Mama C asked. She had gone out during Riley's epic bathroom cleansing and was unwinding a long black scarf from around her neck.

"Fine," Riley answered. In truth, she was nearly vibrating with nervous energy.

Mama C nodded and sat down next to her. The leather cord of the talisman peeked out from beneath her coat.

"What's that?" Riley asked, reaching for the charm.

Mama C's hand flew to her neck, wrapping the talisman in her hand before Riley could touch it. "It's a reminder," she said, voice heavy. "That we can never, ever trust witches."

Riley swallowed hard. "But what is it?"

"It's—" Mama C's hand tightened around the charm. "Old magic," she said, releasing a breath. "Just old magic.

Now, is there anything else you want to tell me about last night?" Mama C said.

This question was a trap. Riley had always known that it was her opportunity to come clean about her wrong-doings, but now that she was a little older, she knew that half the time it was a fishing expedition. Mama C asked the question this way to give Riley the opportunity to confess to things she had no idea Riley had done. When Riley was little, she'd thought Mama C was all-powerful. She now knew that not even Great Cecelia Callahan knew everything.

This time, however, there was plenty to confess, and the first thought to enter Riley's mind was of the hunter. But he wasn't here for wolves. He was here for Ter and as long as she stayed behind the wards, she was safe.

"No," Riley answered solemnly.

"All right." Mama C drew in a deep breath. "Then there's something I want to discuss with you. You are the child of a great pack leader and, like it or not, that comes with certain responsibilities. Can I trust you to bear them?"

"Yes," Riley responded quietly.

"Good. Then there's just one more thing."

Mama C cleared her throat and looked toward the open door. She stood and crossed the room to close it before returning to her spot next to Riley, who was even more nervous than before.

Only two things had ever led to a closed-door conversation in Riley's bedroom. The first had been about Darcy, which hadn't been as confusing as her moms had expected it to be, because Riley had always known that gender was fluid. And the second had been when she'd started her period, which had been superawkward, because it had involved a very detailed book with very detailed pictures and way more information that Riley had been capable of retaining just then.

"We're going to talk about kissing and feelings," Mama C now said, and Riley wished she could disappear into the bed.

"Mom, I know about—"

"I know," Mama C said, cutting her off before she could say the word. "I *know* you do, but if you are sneaking out of the house in the middle of the night, then we need to talk about more than just bodies. We need to talk about feelings."

Riley didn't know where this was going, but she was sure it was somewhere she didn't want to be.

"No matter who you are attracted to, I want to know that you understand that you always have choices and so do they," Mama C continued. "Sometimes being attracted to someone else means the feelings inside us are overwhelming, and that's okay. It's okay to be overwhelmed. The only thing that isn't okay is acting on those feelings without the other person's consent."

Riley thought she was dying. Or maybe she was melting. Face-first. Her cheeks had gotten so hot that they were about to slide off her face.

"Mom," she pleaded.

But Mama C had more to say. "Can you tell me what 'consent' is?"

Riley resisted the urge to fling a quilt over her head. "'Consent' is when you ask someone permission before touching them or invading their physical space."

"Right. So if you feel like you want to kiss someone, what should you do?"

The fact that Riley was having this conversation when she hadn't actually been sneaking out to kiss anyone was mortifying. It was so much worse than knowing Mama C was disappointed in her. She just wanted it to be over.

Still, as she considered the question, she couldn't help but picture a pair of blue eyes staring at her, making her feel something indescribable in her chest.

"I should ask," Riley answered.

"Good." Mama C reached over to cup Riley's cheek in the palm of her hand, the calluses there rough against Riley's skin. "For a long time, wolves like us weren't allowed to choose what happened to their bodies. Thanks to First Wolf, we aren't chained to the cycles of the moon anymore. Choice is our most sacred magic. And it is a gift we give each other. Remember that: choice is your magic and your gift."

It was something Mama C had been telling her all her life, but this time, she felt like she understood it more than she ever had before. No one had given Ter a choice about becoming the Nameless Witch. Surely, Riley's mother would want to help someone in that situation.

"Mom, what would you do if you caught the next Nameless Witch?" Riley asked.

Mama C stiffened. "If we catch her, we'll lock her away where she won't be able to harm any wolves. Ever again."

"But what if she doesn't want to hurt wolves?"

"It doesn't matter," Mama C's response was clipped. "The spell will change her because that's what it does. She may not start off wanting to hurt anyone, but she will."

Riley tried to imagine Ter hurting anyone and couldn't. "How do you know?"

"We know because it has happened before. Even the witches know it will happen again if they don't lock her up. The only reason they informed us was because they can't find her, and they need all the help they can get."

Mama C very rarely got riled up like this. It made Riley nervous, but she had more to ask.

"But what if she didn't *want* to be the Nameless

Witch? What if she ran away because she was looking for help?"

Mama C frowned at her daughter and shook her head. "I'm afraid that doesn't matter. Whether she wants it or not, she is what she is, and I'll do anything to make sure she can't hurt a single wolf."

10

IN WHICH RILEY SNEAKS OUT ON PURPOSE THIS TIME

Later that night, Riley lay in her bed, fully dressed beneath the covers, while she waited for her moms to go to sleep.

She was keenly aware of the irony. Last night, she'd woken up in the woods through no fault of her own and returned home to be busted for sneaking out. Tonight, she was preparing to sneak out. Only this time, she would hopefully not get busted for it.

In a way, she'd already been punished for this exact thing, so really she was just doing things in reverse. Punishment first. Misbehavior second.

Before bedtime, she had carefully pilfered the pantry, grabbing graham crackers and a jar of peanut butter, with several apples and tangerines thrown in for good measure. After that, she'd added one of her sweatshirts, a thick pair socks, and a spare quilt. Then she tried to think of things a witch on the run might need. A toothbrush, because everyone needed a toothbrush, a few jars of herbs for spells, and one of the decorative glass balls from the garden because it seemed like the kind of thing a witch might like. Granted, everything Riley knew about witches, she'd learned from stories like *The Wizard of Oz* and she imagined they were about as accurate as the many werewolf stories she'd heard over the years. Still, she decided to err on the side of too much rather than too little, and she shoved her collection of goods into a bag.

Now, the house was quiet but for the moaning of the wind outside and the soft ticking of the heater. Riley slipped out of bed, retrieved the duffel sack of supplies from her closet, and slowly made her way down the hall to the stairs, where she expertly navigated the squeaks and creaks until she was safely on the first floor. Then it was an easy trip through the front door and down the porch steps, into the night.

In spite of the fact that there were early spring buds sprouting from the tips of tree branches, it was freezing and the air smelled like snow. It wasn't unheard-of for it to snow in Kansas in March, but it would be unusual. Riley longed for the warmer days ahead, but tonight she had the luxury of shoes and appropriate clothing. Still,

Riley shivered as she set the duffel on the ground and closed her eyes. The magic inside her was tingly, and the transformation slid over her skin like a warm coat. Her fingertips sharpened into claws, and she bent forward as her body shifted from two legs to four. She smacked her jaws and stamped her feet, feeling them connect with the cement of the driveway. Then, shoving her nose through the loop of the duffel bag and tossing it onto her back, she began to run.

She knew the way by heart, but everything looked a little different this late at night, when she wasn't supposed to be here.

Riley's neighborhood was on the eastern edge of town where the sidewalks ended abruptly and the houses were spaced farther apart. Streetlights cast an eerie orange glow, leaving Riley feeling exposed. Inside the wards of Wax & Wayne, wolves were protected from being spotted by regular humans. Someone passing nearby would notice a flash of movement and nothing else. Out here, there were no wards to protect her from being seen. There was certainly nothing to protect her from a gunshot. And Mama C had warned Riley to assume that there were always guns nearby.

She abandoned the main road for the yards of her neighbors, where it seemed that each property was equipped with a motion light, tracking her every move.

Riley ran harder, veering away from familiar sights, until she wasn't sure where she was, only that she was running in the right direction.

When she was free of the neighborhood, she paused to take a few deep breaths. Ahead, open fields and country roads invited her to run the rest of the way. But before she could take a step, she sensed something behind her: the quiet snap of a branch under pressure and the barely audible sound of someone breathing.

Shivers vaulted up Riley's spine. She was being watched.

All of her instincts told her to freeze—to crouch low and wait until the danger had passed. But a second *snap* rang through the air, and Riley bolted.

She ran as fast as her body would allow, the sack of supplies bouncing against her back. Right behind her, she could hear someone in pursuit, running hard on her heels.

She had to go faster, but she couldn't. Not with this bag slowing her down, throwing her gait off-kilter.

Her pursuer was catching up, gaining on her with every step. And while she knew that meant that they couldn't be a human or a hunter, fear drove her forward, faster and faster, until her muscles screamed with the effort.

Finally, Riley crossed into Wax & Wayne. She cut through the familiar woods with confidence and speed.

But instead of breaking off at the wards, as she'd expected, her pursuer stayed on her tail. Whoever was following her had to be a wolf, but who?

Then someone rammed into her side, and she crashed to the ground. She slid through the frozen dirt before she came to a stop. Scrabbling to her feet, she tucked her head low and faced her attacker.

A young wolf, with brown fur, white patches over his feet and belly, and a ridiculous open-mouthed grin, stared back at her.

Riley transformed from wolf to girl faster than ever before.

"Milo!" she shouted. "What are you doing out here?"

The transformation shivered over Milo's fur, and he laughed as he shook himself into his human body.

"Does it tickle when you shift, too?" he asked.

"What? No!" Riley answered, exasperated. "Did you follow me?"

"Of course!" Milo narrowed his eyes. "You were being sneaky."

"I was not!"

"You were, and after last night, you have no business being sneaky." His eyes fell instantly to the duffel. "What's in the bag?"

"None of your business," she snapped. "Go home."

"Okay," Milo sang. "But I can't promise that I won't accidentally wake up the moms. And if that happens, I might accidentally turn on the light in your room and they might accidentally notice that you're gone. Again."

Riley ground her teeth. Telling Milo the truth was out of the question, but she had to tell him something. And that something had to be good enough to convince him to go home and leave her alone.

"I'm . . ." Riley paused to consider. There was only one thing that was guaranteed to send Milo racing for home without telling on her. Just thinking about it made Riley's cheeks flush, but she had no other options.

"I'm meeting someone," she said.

"What? But why would you need to sneak out at night to— Oh!" Milo staggered back several paces. "You mean you're meeting a paramour? Gross! Who is it?"

"No. And it's none of your business," Riley responded. "Now go home."

"I am totally going home. No *way* do I want to witness this. But you have to tell me who it is. I bet it's Lydia Edgerton," Milo teased. "Or Luke Shacklett. Or—" Milo stopped suddenly, his eyes tracking something over Riley's shoulder, and he said, "Who are you?"

It was at that exact moment that Riley realized she had led him straight into the heart of Tenderfoot Camp. And standing on the front porch of the cabin they'd claimed for her was none other than Teralyn Grimsley.

SECRETS AND
SECRET KEEPERS

"**O**ooooh, is this your paramour?" Milo asked, in the most obnoxious way possible.

"I don't have a paramour," Riley admitted. "This is no one you need to worry about. Just go home. And if you don't tell on me, I'll do your chores for a week."

Milo narrowed his eyes as he considered this offer. It was a good one. There were few things Milo hated more than chores. But Riley could tell by the way his gaze strayed back to Ter that his curiosity was dangerously close to overwhelming his desire to not do chores.

"What's the big deal? You don't want to introduce me to your friend? Fine, I'll do it myself." He took a step forward and opened his mouth again. "Hi, I'm Mumpfff."

Just in time, Riley had clapped a hand over his mouth, her heart hammering in her ears.

"Don't tell her your name." She waited a second

to make sure Milo knew she wasn't joking. Then she released her hand from his mouth.

"What the heck?" Milo said, a little angry now. "Why can't I tell her my name? Is she a witch or—" Milo nearly gagged. His eyes bugged out wide, and he took a step away from Ter.

"Wait. No way."

"Listen to me." Riley tried to make her voice sound soothing and rational. "No one can know. Not our moms. Not even your prime. No one."

"What?" Milo shook his head in disbelief. "Is this serious? And are you serious?"

Riley nodded once, slowly, before she answered. "This is serious. You cannot. Tell. Anyone."

"But . . ." Milo looked from Riley to Ter and back again. Then he shouted, "She's a witch! Are you dating a witch?"

"I'm not dating a witch!" Riley threw her hands in the air. "I'm not dating anyone. Will you just stop and listen for a minute?"

Milo continued to glower, but he shut up.

"This is Ter. Yes, she's a witch, but she's here because she needs our help." Riley turned to Ter. "Ter, this is my obnoxious little brother. You can call him— Wait. Is it okay if you know first initials?"

Ter nodded. "Just as long as it's not a real nickname. Even nicknames have power. Sometimes even more than birth names."

That made sense to Riley. She could hardly even remember what her sister's name had been before it was Darcy. It probably wouldn't hold that much power over her anymore.

"Okay. Then you can call him Em."

"Nice to meet you, Em," Ter said. "I promise I'm not a bad witch."

Milo pinched his lips shut and didn't speak. At least not to Ter. To his sister, he said, "Why are you helping her?"

Riley considered the question. It was too late to try and convince him this was all a big misunderstanding. But what if he didn't get how important this was? What if he ran straight to their moms? She couldn't risk it. She'd have to settle for part of the truth and hope it held.

"She's run away from home and her coven really wants her back and—"

"WAIT." Milo held his hands out to either side. "Are you telling me that this person right here is the witch everyone is looking for?"

Riley didn't want to answer, but it didn't matter. Milo had already put the pieces together.

"She's the one, isn't she?! She's the Nameless Witch. The next Nameless Witch! And she's here?" Milo looked around as though realizing for the first time where they were. "Why haven't you told our moms?"

"Because it's not as simple as that." Riley tried to

sound calm and like she had everything under control, but she didn't. She really, really didn't.

"Why not?" he asked.

"Because," Riley started. She wished she knew exactly what to say to make him understand. "She doesn't want to be the Nameless Witch. She didn't get to choose it and she's in Lawrence because there's another coven here who might be able to help her. I'm going to help her find them, and in the meantime, she needs a safe place to hide. If we tell our moms they'll lock her up forever. She's just a kid. Like us. And she doesn't deserve that. It's not fair to her."

Milo didn't say anything immediately. He watched Ter through narrowed eyes, but he looked thoughtful. Like he was considering everything Riley had said.

"I understand why you're worried," Ter said, inching forward. "I am, too. I've probably heard all the same stories you have. And the last thing I want to do is put you or your sister in danger. I just need a little help first," she explained.

"We're supposed to tell Mama C if we notice anything," Milo protested, but the fight had gone out of his voice. In spite of himself, he was having a hard time reconciling the smiling face in front of him with visions of the terrible Nameless Witch.

Riley gave him a minute to think, then added, "Two days and then she's gone."

"Two days?" Milo asked, clearly skeptical.

"Two days," Riley confirmed. "Can you keep the secret for that long?"

"From everyone?" Milo looked uncomfortable, like a stone was lodged in his shoe. "I don't know . . ."

It took Riley a beat to understand that it wasn't their moms he was worried about keeping the secret from. It was his prime pack.

One year ago, he would have kept a secret for Riley without a second thought. Even with three years between them, they were close. A united front against the tyranny of their parents.

But there was that distance again. New but somehow already unfathomably wide. In the past few months, while Riley had been forming a bond with her own prime, Milo had been forming one with his. One that meant he was more worried about keeping things from his prime than he was about keeping a secret for his sister. One in which Riley had become Porkenstein the Pig instead of one of the kids who fought against him.

Riley swallowed the small lump in her throat. "Just two days," she repeated.

Milo stared at Ter, who smiled just enough to appear nonthreatening. After a long moment, Milo heaved a sigh and nodded.

"Okay," he said.

"Thank you," Riley said weakly, then turned to Ter

and held up her duffel bag. "I brought you a few things."

Ter pushed open the front door of the cabin to let Riley inside the Yippery.

"Do you want to come in?" Ter asked Milo, peering past Riley's shoulder at him.

"I'm good," Milo said, scuffing a toe in the hard dirt.

"You're welcome if you change your mind," Ter said, but Milo shook his head and plopped down on the front porch.

"I'll wait here," he said, stuffing his hands deep inside his pockets to keep them warm.

"Knock if you change your mind," Riley called as she followed Ter and shut the door behind them.

Inside, the cabin was transformed. Last night, it had been barren and cold, more suited to spiders and mice than to people. Tonight, it was something else entirely.

Long purple curtains hung from the windows, and sparks of purple flame danced around the ceiling. A puffy silver comforter was on one bed, and three soft pillows were stacked against the headboard. The most amazing thing of all was that the room was warm. Outside it was winter-sharp and cold, but inside, it felt like a fire had been burning for hours.

"Do you have a magic bag or something?" Riley said. "And do you always travel with curtains?"

Ter laughed. "No and no. But I can alter things that already exist, make them appear different for a while."

Riley wanted to ask more questions about witch magic, but she also didn't want to appear too interested. Ter was a witch. She wasn't a friend. As soon as this was over, they'd never see each other again.

"Here." Riley thrust the duffel into Ter's hands.

Ter pulled out a jar of dried basil and held it up with a puzzled look on her face. "Is this food?"

"No, that was just to make you feel comfortable," Riley explained.

"In case I . . . missed pasta?"

"I thought— Don't you use herbs in your spells and stuff?" Riley asked, suddenly much less sure of herself.

A smile brightened Ter's face, and Riley thought she was holding herself back from a laugh. "Yes, we do. Not usually like this, but that was really thoughtful of you." She dug a little deeper into the bag and drew out the glass orb Riley had snatched from the front garden.

"Also for magic?" Riley explained, though now that she thought of it, she wasn't so sure witches used crystal balls. Why had she thought that a witch would want an old glass ball that had been sitting in the mud between the coneflowers and the butterfly bush for three years?

Ter collected the globe in her hands and brought it toward her face. She whispered softly, and the ball filled with a purple fog, which slowly parted to reveal a teeny-tiny room. It was dark inside, which made it hard to see, but Riley could make out a bed and a bookshelf, and two windows dressed in purple curtains covered in silver stars.

"What is that?" Riley asked.

"Where," Ter said. "And it's my room. Back home. We can use orbs like this to connect to other scrying surfaces, even if they're miles and miles away. We don't really need them, since we have cell phones now, but it's an old-fashioned way to communicate. Right now, we're looking through the mirror on my dresser."

"Can you use it to find the Free Witches?" Riley asked.

Before Ter could answer, something moved in the tiny room. A shadow drifted across the bed toward the mirror. Ter whispered a few words, and the image of her bedroom vanished.

She shook her head. "It's dangerous to send out a call without knowing who is going to pick up on the other end. I can only connect with my room so easily because it's my mirror and my room." She set the ball down on her bedside table before adding, "There are hubs, sort of like old switchboards for telephones, but I don't think I should try them."

Riley understood what she meant. Ter didn't have anyone to trust. It made Riley's heart squeeze. She remembered when she didn't know who to trust, when the threat of the Devourer had loomed so large that it turned the whole world into a kind of enemy.

"Here," Ter said. "Take this with you."

She dug into her pocket and held out a silver compact between them. It looked old and heavy.

"What's this for?" Riley asked as she popped the compact open and found two mirrors inside.

"So I can call you," Ter explained, gesturing toward her brand-new garden orb. "You know, in case of emergency or something."

Riley pocketed the compact, feeling unsure of herself again, and a little confused as to why. "Cool. Well, I guess I should go."

"One more thing," Ter said, catching Riley's hand in hers. The touch of her skin was soft and warm. "You never told me your name." She shook her head, realizing her mistake. "I mean, what can I call you?"

Riley thought for a minute before she said, "You can call me Winter."

IF YOU GIVE A WITCH YOUR NAME . . .

If you give a witch your name
You know just what she'll do
Once she knows the words to use
She'll play a trick on you
She'll make you think wolves have no tails
Double dee, hubble dee, bubble dee, quick
She'll snip yours off, she will not fail
That's the way of a witch's trick

A PHILOSOPHICAL DIVIDE

With two days remaining on the clock, both of which were school days, there was no time to waste. Luckily, they knew exactly where to find Bethany Books.

The last time Riley and her prime pack had been inside the Clawroot archive, it had been the middle of the night and they'd been searching for any information they could find about the exceptionally scary Devouring Wolf. Maybe it was that memory or maybe it was that books were inherently a little bit creepy, but stepping inside the old building felt to Riley like stepping into a haunted house.

"Why is it always so cold in here?" Aracely said.

"It's winter," Dhonielle answered irritably. "It's cold everywhere."

"No. My house is warm," Aracely said. "And the dining hall is warm when the ovens are on. But I guess school is pretty cold. I think I've worn this Sherpa hoodie for three weeks straight."

At that, everyone paused to look at her. The garment in question was bright orange and fuzzy, with two panda ears on the hood, one of which bent forward while the other stood straight up. It made her look a little bit confused all the time, which was probably accurate.

"Aracely," Lydia said sweetly, "I'm going to tell you something, and please don't take this the wrong way, but we know. We can smell it. That hoodie is growing sentient life at this point, and you must wash it."

"Or set it on fire," Kenver muttered.

"Rude," Aracely said as she surreptitiously sniffed an underarm and wrinkled her nose in distaste.

"Bethany is probably in the back," Riley said, taking the lead on the real task at hand.

Light streamed in through high windows as they walked between stacks of old books and binders. There were labels carved into wooden plaques, which said things like MUNDANE LORE and SELENOLOGY and MODERN MAGIC. Each sat on a shelf with a lot of books that looked like they were much older than Riley and a few that were obviously brand-new. The internet age had been good for the packs. They could compile and share information with the click of a few buttons, instead of having to design, print, and publish everything themselves.

"Fee, fie, foe, fack, who's that shuffling through my stacks?" The voice of Bethany Books came to them from the very depths of the archive.

They spotted her at a desk piled high with books and notebooks, and what appeared to be an old flower vase stuffed with rolled-up maps. Rather, they spotted the bright blue rims of her glasses peering over a haphazardly arranged stack of books.

"Just us," Riley said. Then, afraid that Bethany might not be able to see them, she added, "Riley, Dhonielle, Lydia, Kenver, and Aracely."

"And what brings such renowned mischief-makers to my door?" Bethany asked as she came around to the front of her desk. She was dressed to match her glasses, in a teal turtleneck sweater and a long blue skirt, which swept the tops of her toes. They were visible in tan sandals, her toenails painted a creamy yellow.

"Um, Ms. Books," Riley said, with a frown, "aren't your feet cold?"

"My personal philosophy is that you have to dress for the weather you want," Bethany said. "Not the weather you have."

"That doesn't make any sense," Kenver grumbled.

"Once the weather knows it can beat you, it will become a tyrant." Bethany flashed a broad smile at their skeptical faces. "You'll learn soon enough. Now, what can I do for you today?"

"We have a few questions about witches," Dhonielle said.

"Witches?" Bethany's eyes widened in surprise. "I

guess it's no surprise, given the recent news, but with you five . . . ? Should I be suspicious?"

"Probably," Kenver offered, without any hint of humor.

"We're just curious," Riley hurried to add. They were encouraged to ask questions whenever they had them, but the last thing they needed was Bethany reporting back to Mama C. It was best to keep things as casual as possible. "The news made us realize that we don't know as much as we thought."

Bethany's laughter was warm and bright—completely incongruous with the chilly, dim archive. "I appreciate your honesty," she said. "All right, hit me. What do you want to know about witches?"

This was the part Riley always struggled with. She knew what she wanted to ask, but how to ask it in a way that wouldn't get her prime pack into some kind of hot water was another thing altogether. It was like trying to tell someone the sky was blue without using the word *blue*.

Luckily, Dhonielle never seemed to have that problem.

"The emergency forum got us thinking," she started. "We grew up hearing that Wax & Wayne was safe. But how safe is it? It's a secret from most humans, but what about witches and hunters? Do they know where we are?"

"It's true that it's difficult"—Bethany nodded tentatively—"maybe even impossible, to keep the location of a pack like ours secret. So we've always operated on the assumption that it isn't. Instead, we focus on finding ways to keep our pack safe, informed, and capable of defending themselves against many kinds of dangers."

"So that's a yes?" Dhonielle asked.

Bethany confirmed it with a nod. "Many of them do . . ." she said.

"Ugh." Aracely shuddered, in her fuzzy, dirty hoodie. "I did *not* need to know that."

"What about the Free Witches of Lawrence?" Dhonielle continued, ignoring Aracely. "Do they know where we are? And if they do, do we know where *they* are?"

"You mean do we have an understanding of mutually assured destruction?" asked Bethany. "If they hurt us, we'll hurt them, and vice versa?"

Here, Dhonielle faltered.

"Something like that," Riley said, stepping in. Now that Dhonielle had opened the door, Riley knew how to get them through it. "We were just thinking that we don't know very much about witches at all. Except that we can't trust them."

"My mama says they're evil," Aracely said.

Bethany raised a finger in the air, as if in protest.

"They're not evil?" Riley said.

"'Evil' is such a subjective term, really. To worms, birds are evil. To bunnies, wolves are. And to the earth itself, all humanity probably seems a little bit evil." Bethany pressed a hand to her mouth briefly, as though attempting to silence herself, before starting again. "Witches and wolves have a complicated relationship, but it's not a question of good and evil so much as it is a tangled web of history and experience. We have wildly different approaches to magic, for example, and that has created a seemingly impenetrable philosophical divide."

"What kind of differences?" Kenver seemed interested for the first time since arriving in the archive.

Bethany's whole demeanor seemed to shift at that question, going from slightly suspicious to conspiratorial in the blink of an eye. Sometimes it was easy to forget that, in her early twenties, she was closer to their age than she was to their parents'.

"For starters," she said, "they control when a young witch comes into their power."

"What? How?" Kenver's voice was just the slightest bit angry.

"Well, every young witch has the potential for magic inside them—just like wolves—but they can't express that potential and use their magic until they undergo a ritual. It's not entirely dissimilar to the Full Moon Rite. In fact, we think the origins are similar. But in our case, or in most of our cases, the entry into full wolf magic is more organic. Whereas in the case of witches, it needs to be unlocked by their coven."

"So witches can't reach their magic without a coven?"

Kenver's frown had only deepened. "What happens if the coven just doesn't like you? You never get to use your own magic?"

"And that is at the heart of our philosophical divide. They do this because in the past it was very dangerous for a witch to come into their powers without other witches there to support them, especially if they were in public when it happened. It led to the death of many young witches, in fact, and so they came up with a spell that would allow them to control when a young witch would come into their power. It was the same spell, in fact, that created the first Nameless Witch. At least, that's the common theory. Something about consolidation of magic," Bethany said. Then seeing that Kenver was still waiting for an answer, she added, "Yes, that is what it means."

Riley didn't like the thought of that at all. It had been hard enough when the five of them hadn't transformed at the Full Moon Rite, like their peers. If that had happened because other wolves had power over that transformation, because they were choosing for them, it would have been infinitely worse.

Riley thought of Mama C's words from the night before: *Choice is our most sacred magic.* It was starting to make a little more sense now. Ter was running from her coven because they had made a choice for her. One she didn't agree with and wanted to change. It was hard to imagine that happening in Riley's pack.

"That's horrible," Lydia mused. "Are all witches like that? Do they all believe the same things?"

"Definitely not. Remember, it's because of a witch that we even have the Full Moon Rite, so we weren't always so polarized. In fact, the Free Witches of Lawrence are known to be a bit more progressive than their conservative counterparts. They were among the first to break with traditional gender expectations—which was huge back in the day. Of course, they have more reason than most to take a critical look at the way things are."

Riley could tell that Bethany was about to take a much deeper dive into witch history than they needed at the moment.

"Do you know where the Free Witches are?" Riley asked.

"I—" Bethany blinked in surprise. "Why?"

That seemed like a confirmation to Riley. "Shouldn't we all know?" She hoped the question sounded more innocent than she felt asking it.

"It might at least be helpful to know the places to avoid," Lydia added.

Bethany narrowed her eyes, but she didn't shut the line of questioning down immediately, which Riley took as a good sign.

"Also, if we have a special destruction treaty or whatever, isn't it just better to know where they might be?" Aracely said. "It would suck to be getting a new pair of earrings and accidentally step on a witch's foot or some-thing, and—" She jolted upright. "Claws and teeth! Do you think they run the Claire's Boutique downtown? I would totally run a jewelry shop if I were a witch."

"They don't run the Claire's," Bethany said dismissively. "They wouldn't be caught dead in a place like that. Especially not with a coffee shop so nearby. That is their—"

"They're in La Prima Tazza?" said Riley, louder than she'd intended.

Bethany's mouth snapped shut. She puffed up her cheeks before blowing out a breath. "I suppose a prime like you would have found out anyway. Just promise me you'll be careful."

"I promise," Riley said, trying to contain the urge to grin. "Thank you."

Riley couldn't believe their luck. They'd solved the first piece of this puzzle, and tomorrow they would go out and find a witch.

13

A NAMELESS WITCH

Being inside the Raven Book Store in downtown Lawrence felt like being inside a treasure chest. The walls were painted in bright candy colors, and everywhere Riley turned there was a secret nook with an old-fashioned chair tucked into a corner, some of which were currently occupied by cats.

Dhonielle's dad, Uncle Will, had worked here as long as Riley could remember. He did everything from recommending books to eager readers to making sure the cats were fed to welcoming fancy authors in to talk about whatever it was fancy authors talked about.

Riley had never been more excited that her uncle worked in a bookstore, because it gave her and Dhonielle the perfect excuse to be downtown after school the very next day. All she'd had to do was ask Mama N if she could go home with Dhonielle instead of taking the bus, and it was a done deal.

"Hey, girls," Uncle Will said as they came through the

back door. "I need about thirty minutes. Think you can find something to occupy your time?"

"We're going to run down the street for a latte at LPT," Riley said brightly.

"Oh." Uncle Will had clearly been expecting another answer. He leaned forward, pressing his forearms to the counter; his long, silvering locs fell over his shoulder. His skin was darker than Dhonielle's, more earthy black than warm brown, but their eyes were exactly the same. Big and bright and the soft brown of an oak tree. "I thought coffee didn't happen until you were sixteen. Did I get that wrong?"

Dhonielle smirked. "Dad, stop playing."

Uncle Will winked at his daughter and stood up straight. "Be back in"—he checked his phone—"twenty-six minutes. Okay?"

They agreed and were out the door a second later.

The walk to La Prima Tazza was short, but it was freezing outside, the winter wind sharpening off the river, and by the time they reached the small coffee shop, their noses were numb and Riley couldn't feel her toes. They paused just inside the door, taking in the tables packed with students and professors and townies, all with steaming mugs of coffee, stacks of books, or open laptops before them. The air smelled rich and nutty, with a dash of sugar that made Riley's mouth water.

"That walk took us three minutes." Dhonielle had

started a countdown on her phone. She held it up so Riley could see their time draining away. "Only twenty-three minutes left."

"That's plenty of time," Riley said, but the seconds seemed to be ticking by much faster than she thought they should.

They approached the counter, where large chalkboards listed dozens of drinks, organized first by type—coffee or tea—and then by temperature—hot or cold. The thought of ordering something cold right now seemed completely bonkers to Riley, so she focused on the hot menu.

She didn't have much experience with coffee. Her moms made a pot every morning, and even Darcy had started drinking it, but without copious amounts of added milk and sugar, Riley didn't see the appeal. Here, though, there were drinks called the Snow Tiger and the Mole Mocha, which sounded like things Riley might want to taste.

"She definitely looks like a witch," Dhonielle whispered, pressing close to Riley's side and nodding toward the girl behind the counter.

Riley blinked. She'd been so taken in by the drink descriptions that she'd almost forgotten what they'd come here for.

The barista *did* look like a witch. She was short, with a long braid of midnight hair and skin that was tan. She wore dramatic eye makeup, which was both sharp and bright, and her fingers were covered with interesting rings, which didn't look like the sort of thing one would find at a regular jewelry store. She grinned at them, and when she spoke, her voice was thick and sweet, like honey.

"What can I get for you two?"

"Um . . ." Dhonielle's mouth fell open, as though all rational thought had just abandoned her.

"Two Mole Mochas, please," Riley said, without thinking.

"Good choice. That's a house specialty," the girl said. "It's a little spicy, though. You good with that?"

Riley nodded hurriedly and elbowed Dhonielle in the ribs. She didn't need to speak, but she did need to shut her mouth.

"Do you think she puts potions into these drinks?" Dhonielle whispered, in sudden alarm. "It would be the perfect cover for a witch's brew!"

"Shhh." Riley elbowed her cousin a second time. But the barista couldn't hear them over the sound of her machines grinding coffee beans and steaming milk. The air filled with the scents of coffee and chocolate and chili peppers.

"Sorry," Dhonielle murmured. "I'm just so nervous. She's a real, live witch, and the only thing I've ever heard about witches is that they like to trap wolves and use their parts for magic. And in case you've forgotten, *we* are the wolves in this scenario."

Riley cast a look around the coffee shop for anyone who might have overheard.

Riley turned to face her cousin. "She won't know we're wolves unless someone shouts it at her!"

Dhonielle opened her mouth, then snapped it shut again. "Sorry," she whined.

"Remember what Bethany said. The Free Witches are a progressive coven. And we have a sort of treaty with them. They won't enspell us in a coffee shop, where anyone can see."

"Yeah. Okay." Dhonielle took a deep breath and made a visible effort to calm down.

Just then, the girl swiveled around with a tall cup in each hand. She set the steaming-hot drinks on the counter and covered them in generous piles of whipped cream, topped with sprinkles of cinnamon and nutmeg.

"Here you go," she said, with a friendly smile. "That'll be nine dollars and sixty-three cents."

As Riley paid, she tried to think of a natural way to ask this girl if she was a witch. She wished they had more time, but not only was Uncle Will's deadline approaching, the line was growing behind them. It was now or never.

Riley leaned in close and kept her voice low when she asked, "Excuse me, but are you one of the Free Witches?"

"Of course," she girl said with a laugh, which raised Riley's hopes. They were dashed almost as quickly when the girl gave them a wink and added, "All witches are free witches."

The next customer stepped up to the counter, and the girl went about her business—making coffee drinks and, apparently, not being a Free Witch. Riley felt like her feet were frozen to the floor. This was their only lead, their only chance to find a witch who might be willing to help Ter. If this didn't work, Riley didn't know what to try next.

"Nine minutes," Dhonielle said. She didn't sound nearly as disappointed as Riley felt. They both wanted to help Ter.

"They have to be here." Riley knew she was being stubborn, and she didn't care. "If Bethany said there are witches here, then there are witches here. We just need more time to find them."

"Well, we have eight minutes." Dhonielle tugged at Riley's sleeve. "Maybe there's another way to find the witches."

"Witches can only be found when they *want* to be found."

Riley and Dhonielle froze. The voice had come from behind. Very close behind.

Panic tickled up and down Riley's spine, but she turned around to face the eavesdropper. She found a

young man standing only a foot away. She noticed his sculpted blond hair first, because it looked like a crown. Then she noticed his eyes. They were pale brown, almost unnaturally so, and combined with his cool, ivory skin, they gave him the appearance of a ghost.

"I didn't mean to startle you, but I hear the word 'witch' and my paranormal detection senses start tingling." He shrugged. "Besides, you weren't exactly being subtle."

Riley glared at her cousin from the corner of her eye. "Why do you know about witches?"

"Oh, apologies. I thought that was obvious." He opened his arms and gave a little bow. "I am one."

Dhonielle gasped. Riley didn't blame her. This was shocking news. Apart from being dressed in head-to-toe black, this boy looked nothing like a witch. He had short hair and wore no jewelry that they could see. If anything, he resembled a member of a boy band from the '90s.

"*You're* a witch?" Riley said, doing her best to keep her voice down.

"At your service."

"Six minutes," Dhonielle said softly.

Riley did the math her in her head. Six minutes on the clock. They'd need three of them to get back to the Raven Book Store. There was no time to waste.

"Can you get us in touch with the Free Witches?" Riley asked.

"Maybe." The boy's smile turned teasing and

suspicious. "But if I were going to do that, I'd need to know why two little pups like you are trying to make friends with witches. What is it that you need?"

Dhonielle's fingers curled into the sleeve of Riley's coat, and she squeezed. Hard. Riley had heard it, too. He'd called them pups. He *must* be a witch.

Riley swallowed the lump of fear in her throat. "We need your help. We—" She shared a look with Dhonielle. They hadn't discussed exactly what they would say, and now that the moment was here, Riley struggled to find the words.

"There's a witch who needs your help," Dhonielle supplied. "She has a big problem and can only trust the Free Witches."

Riley nodded, glad that Dhonielle was with her after all. She always knew how to explain complicated situations.

"Why doesn't she come herself?" he asked.

"She can't," Riley said quickly. "There's a hunter after her, so she can't come out in the open."

The boy raised an eyebrow. "A hunter? That sounds serious."

"Serious enough for us to come looking for witches," Dhonielle said.

The boy tipped his head in response. "Touché," he said.

"Will you help?" Riley asked.

"First, tell me this: Why do you want to help her?"

"Because . . ." Riley didn't feel comfortable giving him

the real reason: that helping Ter would help wolves. Telling him that it was the right thing to do might make her sound too young or naive. But there was another reason, one she hadn't considered until now. "She doesn't have anyone else to help her."

The boy thought for a minute before digging a hand into the pocket of his black peacoat and withdrawing a copper coin three times the size of a quarter. He offered it to Riley, dropping it into her palm. It was heavier than she'd expected, with a brassy finish and designs stamped into either side.

"Give that to her," he said, beginning to walk away. "She'll know what to do."

"Wait . . ." Riley started, but Dhonielle held up the phone. They had less than three minutes left. They were going to have to run.

Riley followed her cousin out of the warm coffee shop into the winter wind. As they raced down Mass Street, carefully balancing their coffee cups, past clusters of college kids, families with dogs, and a man playing a saxophone at one corner, Riley realized something odd: the boy had offered his help but never his name.

14

A CALL IN THE DARK

There was no escaping the house that night. First of all, everyone was home for dinner, and second of all, Riley's moms decided to settle in with a movie, which didn't even start until eight o'clock.

Riley climbed into bed with the witch's coin in her hand. She turned it over and over, studying the designs on each side. On one, an image of a river snaking away beneath a crescent moon. On the other, a crest with the letters FWC written in slashing calligraphy. She assumed the initials stood for *Free Witch Coven*.

"Winter?"

Riley palmed the coin and sat up. Her room was dark and empty, but for her cat Cottonwood, already coiled in sleep at the foot of her bed.

"Winter?" the voice called again, hissing but also muffled.

"Hello?" Riley whispered to the empty room. "Ter?"

"Here! I mean, in here. The mirror!"

Riley looked at the mirror that leaned against her wall, but there was nothing there. Just a dim reflection of the end of her bed and the window behind it.

"Um, what?" Riley asked the air.

"I mean the compact," Ter said. "The one I gave you?"

"Oh!" Riley grabbed it from her bedside table and popped it open.

There, on the round mirror, no bigger than an apple, was Ter's face. She was surrounded by that same purple smoke from before, puffing around the edges like clouds.

"Hi," Riley said, smiling automatically.

"Hi." Ter smiled back, then frowned. "Oh, I didn't mean to wake you up."

"You didn't," Riley assured her.

"I just . . . Well, it's been nearly three full days, and I wanted to see if you'd had any luck or if I needed to . . . to . . ."

Even though Ter's face was only two inches high on the mirror, Riley could see how scared she was. It made Riley feel terrible that she hadn't tried harder to update her.

"We found the Free Witches," she blurted out. "Well, we found a Free Witch. We didn't have time to get his name, but we did get this coin thingy." She held it up for Ter to see. "He said you'd know what to do with it."

"That's great! So great! Thank you," Ter said with a laugh. "I can use that to contact him."

"Cool," Riley said, tucking the coin inside her pillow-case for safekeeping. "I know I said three days but, considering the circumstances, you can have a little more time. We'll bring the coin to you tomorrow afternoon. After school and some wolf stuff we can't skip."

"Thank you." Ter nodded, and it was hard to tell, but Riley thought she could see tears in her eyes.

"Sure," Riley said, feeling awkward and confused. She didn't understand how her mom could want to lock up someone like Ter, who hadn't done anything wrong. It seemed cruel and unfair, and even though Riley loved her mom, she didn't feel bad about disobeying her now. And that was very, very confusing.

"I'm sorry if I made things difficult with your brother," Ter said. "He seems really sweet."

Riley snorted. "You must not have any brothers."

Ter shook her head. "Just an older cousin, but he's not what I would call 'sweet.'"

"Well, trust me, younger brothers are the actual worst. And recently, he's been obsessed with the idea that I'm dating someone."

"He thought it might be me?" Ter asked, sounding surprised.

Riley didn't answer right away. Sometimes she forgot that there were people in the world who weren't like her. Who didn't like it when girls liked girls or people who they thought looked like boys weren't boys. She didn't worry about it so much in the pack, but Ter wasn't a wolf. She was essentially a stranger.

Still, Ter didn't sound upset, only curious.

"Yeah," she said. "He did."

Ter laughed again, and it eased a little knot of tension out of Riley's lungs, until she was laughing, too. Quietly, though, to avoid attracting the attention of her brother.

"You're pretty lucky," Ter said when they'd stopped their giggles. "He clearly cares about you."

Riley's first reaction was to deny it. Milo had been acting like a monster. He was obsessed with his prime. So much so that he read what Teddy read and had started to think what Teddy thought. Even about her. Riley didn't know how to think about that, but she did know that she'd still do anything for her little brother.

"He's okay," she admitted.

"He likes you for who you are," Ter said. "That's more than okay."

Riley wondered if there was anyone in the world who cared about Teralyn Grimsley for who she was. Some people wanted to catch her so she could become the Nameless Witch and be locked up forever, others wanted to stop her by some equally horrible means, but was there anyone who cared about who Ter really was right now?

Thinking about it made Riley feel guilty, because she was one of the people who only cared about what Ter would or wouldn't become.

Wasn't she?

"Why don't you want to be the Nameless Witch?" Riley said. "I know I asked you before, but it seems pretty important to witches."

The mirror seemed to go blurry for a second, and when it came back into focus, Ter wasn't smiling anymore. Riley wondered if the strength of witches' magic was connected to their emotions.

"What do you know about the Nameless Witch?" Ter asked.

"Not much," Riley admitted. "I know that she's powerful and that when she learns a wolf's true name, she can control them. Make them forget who they are. Do you . . . I mean, is that true?"

Ter nodded. "I think so. But they weren't all like that, and it's not why the first Nameless Witch became nameless."

"Why, then?"

"A long time ago, people were so frightened of witches that they searched for them, hunted them, and sometimes killed them."

"The witch trials," Riley said. "We learned about them in history."

Ter nodded somberly. "It happened because young witches had no way of controlling when they came into their powers. Or how."

"What does that mean?" Riley asked.

"Witches come into their power between the ages of nine and twelve, but before the Nameless Witch, we didn't know exactly when it would happen," Ter explained. "That was dangerous, because when it happens, it's kind of obvious."

"Obvious how?"

"It's beautiful, really." Ter's eyes focused on some far-away memory, and her expression softened. "There's a blossoming of light that we can feel growing. It's like a gentle sun is rising in our chest. And then we fly! Not very high and not for very long, but our bodies know what to do before we do, and we just kind of float for a minute. Which is great when we can plan for it, but it used to just happen. One minute a witch could be out doing something like going to market or sitting in church, and the next . . ."

Riley quickly understood the potential danger of the situation. "It would be like a tenderfoot pup trans-forming for the first time while they were tending the chickens or something. But that could never happen to us, because First Wolf made it so that even if we don't know what year our first transformation will occur, we do know it will happen on the first full moon of summer. We're always prepared."

"Exactly," Ter said. "Witches needed something like

that to keep them safe, but there was so much secrecy between witches that many had no idea they had any magic at all until it was too late."

"You mean there weren't always covens?" Riley asked. As far as she knew, there had always been wolf packs. Even before First Wolf cast the spell that untethered their transformations from the full moon. And weren't covens just witch packs?

"There were, but it wasn't always safe for them to meet or speak. They were intensely secretive, because once accusations of witchcraft started to fly, there was no telling who would turn on whom."

"So what did they do?" Riley asked.

Ter's image shifted, and Riley imagined her sitting on her puffy comforter, surrounded by purple curtains, in the Yippery.

"A very clever witch decided that the best way to keep young witches safe was by controlling when they received their powers. If the older ones had control, they could make sure young witches came into their powers safely. But to do that, they needed a vessel. One witch who could become the focal point of all witch magic in the land." Ter pressed her lips tightly together. "So that's what she did. She created a spell that rerouted every stream and river of magic so that it flowed through her."

"That's a lot of power for one person," Riley said.

"It is. And the spell was so powerful that it filled her

up entirely. The magic needed every bit of her body and mind. It pushed everything else out. Even her name. At least that's the way the story goes."

"She sacrificed herself," Riley said softly. Though she had never heard the story before, it felt familiar. "To protect all the witches who would come after her. Just like First Wolf did for us."

"She did," Ter confirmed, her voice small and quiet.

"But what does this have to do with you?" Riley asked.

Ter's lips puckered and twisted, like she didn't want to say any more. Riley's stomach clenched in response, leaving a nervous feeling, fluttering there like a trapped butterfly.

Finally, Ter answered. "There have been nine Nameless Witches since the first. There must always be a Nameless Witch. And as one nears the end of her life, the next Nameless Witch is chosen. When the transfer occurs, that new witch gives up everything. They become more powerful than any other living witch, but they live in captivity for the rest of their life."

Now, as understanding settled in Riley's mind, her stomach did more than clench. She suddenly felt like she might vomit. "Why?" she said.

"You already know part of this story." Ter inhaled slowly. "The eighth Nameless Witch was one of the Free Witches. No one knows exactly why, but she became obsessed with wolves. She discovered that she could control them and force them to bend to her will. She made them do terrible things, and then she used their bones in her magic. But it wasn't only wolves. Eventually, she became so hungry for power that she turned on witches, too. That was when they locked her up in a tower. After that, they decided to lock up every Nameless Witch in the future. Because I guess once the spell takes effect, they become hungry for more and more magic, the way she was. It's like the spell itself changed over time."

"That's horrible," Riley whispered. "Why hasn't anyone tried to change it?"

"I don't know," Ter said helplessly. "But the spell is already in place, and it will be complete at the exact moment of the spring equinox if I can't find some way to stop it." Even in the dark, Riley could see the glimmer of tears in Ter's eyes as she said this.

Riley felt sick. And maybe angry, too. This went against everything her moms had ever told her about magic. She knew this was witch business and she shouldn't care, but as she watched Ter fight against her tears, Riley realized that she did care. And not just because helping Ter helped all wolves. Not just because it was the right thing to do. She cared about helping Ter.

"What is something you like or like to do?" Riley asked.

Ter blinked at the change in topic. "I love to fly. It's my favorite thing in the whole world. And . . ." She dragged out the word as she considered. Then her face broke into the biggest smile Riley had seen on her yet and she added, "Have you ever used a Twizzler to drink a Coke? If you bite off both ends, it's like a straw, and then when you combine that with Coke? Perfection."

"That sounds gross, but I definitely want to try it," Riley said, laughing a little.

"Riley?" Mama N's voice was right outside the door.

"I have to go!" whispered Riley. She snapped the compact shut just as her bedroom door swung open.

15

GREAT-UNCLE JACK

"Riley?" Mama N said again. "Who are you talking to?"

"No one," Riley answered. "Just . . . to myself."

Mama N came all the way into the room and sank down onto the edge of Riley's bed. The light from the hallway spilled around her head like a halo.

"CeCe does that sometimes, too," she said, stroking a soft hand over Riley's cheek. "She says it helps her organize her thoughts."

Riley liked when Mama N compared her to Mama C. Even if she hadn't actually been talking to herself this time. She did have a lot of thoughts to get in order. About Ter and the Nameless Witch, about witches in general. But also about other things.

"Mom," she said, "why does Mama C hate witches so much?"

Mama N was silent for a few seconds before answering.

"It's complicated, but in a way it's also very simple.

Her parents—your grandparents—were terrified of witches. They grew up in the years just after the Nameless Witch wreaked havoc on this community. I'm sure you've heard of your great-uncle Jack."

"I know he died when Mom was really young," Riley replied.

"Yes, well, the full story is . . . terrible."

"What happened?" Riley asked, trying not to seem overeager.

"It's not really a bedtime story, Riley." Mama N started to leave, but Riley caught her hand.

"But don't you think I should know?" she said. "Does it have something to do with witches? If it does, shouldn't you tell me so I have all the information I need to make informed choices for me and my pack?"

Even in the dark, Riley could see the way Mama N narrowed her eyes suspiciously. "I know you're just trying to stay up late, but that is a good argument, so I'll tell you the short version. Scoot over."

Riley made room on the bed, then settled against Mama N's slight frame, pressing an ear to her chest so she could feel the vibration of her voice as she spoke.

"It does have to do with witches. More than that, though, it has to do with the Nameless Witch." Mama N paused and for a second Riley worried that she'd changed her mind. Then she took a breath and continued. "They say that the Nameless Witch caught your great-uncle

Jack when they were both still quite young. He wasn't any older than fifteen when she found him and learned his name. But she didn't take him right away. Instead, she would call to him when she needed something. And because she knew his name, he would do whatever she told him to. His will belonged to her. So if she told him to smile, he'd smile. And if she told him to bring her another young wolf, he'd do that, too."

Riley imagined it and shuddered. "Couldn't he tell someone?"

Mama N shook her head. "Not if she'd told him not to. He didn't have any choice in the matter. And she used him like this for years. Until one day, she decided that she needed more, and she told him to transform into his wolf form so that she could snip off his tail."

That made Riley flinch, and she squeezed her eyes shut to ward off the image that sprang to mind. "Ugh" was all she could say.

"I told you it was a terrible story. And it didn't end well. Let's just say that the Nameless Witch decided wolf bones made the best magic. She would turn them into charms and talismans and who knows what else. Most of them are still out there somewhere, but every so often one makes its way back to the pack."

Riley pictured the talisman hanging around Mama C's neck. The talisman made from her great-uncle's bones.

Her stomach felt queasy. "No wonder Mama C hates witches."

Mama N climbed out of bed and tucked the quilt up around Riley's shoulders. "I won't speak for her, but I will say that sometimes what looks like hate is actually fear. Maybe it's wearing an intimidating mask, but it's very different from real hate."

With that, Mama N leaned down and planted a kiss on Riley's forehead. Then she wished her good night and left.

THE BOOM CALL

The next day after school, all six of the prime packs in Riley's cohort were in Clawroot, gathered in their usual practice field with Great Callahan.

Riley hadn't been able to stop thinking about Mama N's words from the night before. She'd known Ter's situation was bad, but she hadn't known how bad. She was even more anxious to get the coin to Ter so that Ter could contact the Free Witches and get the help she needed.

"We're going to do something a little different today," Great Callahan began. "Something a little exciting and a little tricky. We're going to practice the Boom Call."

There was a murmur of excitement. The Boom Call was big wolf magic, something they weren't supposed to learn until every member of their prime was twelve years old. For a wolf like Milo, that wasn't for three more years.

"I know it's early for many of you, but given our current circumstances, it's prudent that we move more quickly than usual." Great Callahan's breath puffed white as she spoke. "We don't expect trouble, but it is always best to be prepared. Especially when it comes to witches. Especially when it comes to the Nameless Witch."

Riley noticed Milo watching her intently. She ignored him.

"So who can tell me what kind of magic we use for the Boom?"

Kenver's hand shot up so fast Riley was surprised they didn't come off the ground.

"Yes, Kenver?"

"Acoustics," Kenver said confidently. "You match your tone to the inherent resonance of another item, then use that resonance to change its state."

"That's right." Great Callahan looked impressed. Riley swelled with a little pride for her packmate.

"I don't understand," Teddy said. "Acoustics is sound and force. It's not alchemy. It doesn't change things."

"You're thinking about it as a single thing. One that comes from you," Great Callahan explained patiently. "Instead, think about acoustics as something that exists everywhere. The bits that come from you are just one expression of it, but everything—every animal, every stone, every tree or flower or blade of grass—is a part of a choir of sound resonating all around us, even if we can't always hear the individual notes."

"If you can't hear them, then how do you know they're there?" pressed Teddy, blue eyes narrowing. "Is it magic?"

"Good question. And, no, it's not magic. It's science. But science and magic are best friends. They make each other better. And sometimes it takes a little bit of science to unlock what our magic is capable of."

She scooped up a large sack that had been slouched on the ground behind her and began to empty its contents. It was a collection of random items: a couple of plastic fidget spinners, a few apples, a coffee mug, a stuffed animal, a horseshoe, and chunk of wood carved into the shape of a howling wolf head.

"I want each prime to select one item and then spread out," she said. "Find a place where you can circle up and work together."

"Dibs!" Aracely dove forward before anyone could stop her and snatched the stuffed animal from the pile.

She returned with a satisfied smile on her face and what appeared to be a teddy bear clutched tightly to her chest. Or at least that's what it had once been. Its fur was matted or completely rubbed away in places, and it was missing both of its ears.

"You realize you're hugging a dog toy, right?" Dhonielle said. "And it's covered in germs and microbes and who knows what else."

"Those are all love marks," Aracely said. Then she raised the love-marked bear and nuzzled its nose with her own.

"It's a good choice," Lydia said before Dhonielle could protest further.

"Over there," Riley said, eyeing an open spot by the edge of the clearing.

"No way," Teddy said. "We saw it first!" He shouldered past Riley and hurried ahead to claim the spot.

"Hey!" shouted Aracely. "That was *our* spot, and you know it!"

"So we should just give it to you?" Teddy said. "Because you're the Winter Pack?"

"We never said that," Riley said, scowling deeply.

"Prove it, then."

Riley could feel the eyes of all the other prime packs on the two of them. He was daring her to take the spot and prove his point.

I can kick him in the nuts, Aracely offered. *I've done it before. I know how.*

But Riley's eyes fell on Milo. Getting into a fight with his alpha wasn't doing him any favors. They were going to have to figure this out another way.

"We'll find somewhere better," Riley announced, turning on her heel.

The only place left was right in the middle. Where everyone would be able to see what they were doing. Her cheeks were hot and her brain buzzed with irritation. As she led her pack to the middle of the grove, it felt like everyone was still watching them. It seemed that no matter what they did, they were on the outside. People viewed them as different because of something completely out of their control. Just like Ter. And it wasn't fair.

Before Riley could worry about it more, Great Callahan announced that it was time to begin.

"It will be easier if you can work together," she said as she paced through the clearing. "Place your object in the center of your pack. Then match the tone of your call so that you're all singing the same note. Alphas, you'll need to change the tone until you feel it connect with the object. It should feel like two magnets clicking together. Right now, that's all I want you to do. Find the frequency of your object and match it."

Riley stared at the stuffed animal Aracely had placed on the ground in the center of their circle. Then she blew out a breath, drew in a new one, and picked a note. The others matched it, filling the air with their voices, but the toy bear merely gazed up at the sky with its black marble eyes. There was no magnetic click.

All around, the other five prime packs were howling as they tried to discover the frequency of their objects.

Riley picked a new note, moving up the scale by half steps the way she'd learned in music class at school. This time, she could tell even before the others matched her that it was the wrong frequency, so she changed again, sliding up the scale by two whole steps.

Does that tickle anyone else? Aracely asked.

Dhonielle and Kenver both nodded, and Lydia began to smile. They were close, and they could all feel it.

Full of excitement now, Riley changed her tone just a fraction, easing her voice higher by the barest bit. The others followed her lead and, suddenly, they felt it. The click of their frequency matching that of the stuffed bear on the ground. It came with a surge of power, their five voices linking together as one, the magic of their call growing exponentially.

It felt amazing. Like they could hold this note forever. Riley could see her own wonder reflected in the eyes of the others. Their voices grew louder, more powerful.

And then, the bear wasn't on the ground anymore but rising into the air. It drifted up, up, up, until it was hovering three feet above their heads. Their voices grew louder, pushing it even higher into the sky, and then—*BOOM!*

The bear exploded, raining cottony white fluff down onto their heads.

They'd done it! Not only had they found the right frequency, but they'd used it to change the bear's state.

"Very good. Well done, pups." Great Callahan's praise was subdued, but somehow that made it all the sweeter.

Riley beamed. But her joy was short-lived. When she looked away from the destroyed bear to the other prime packs, she saw that none of the other groups had been able to find the right frequency. And they were all looking at the Winter Pack with what Riley realized was jealousy.

None more so than Teddy Griffin.

IF YOU GIVE A WITCH YOUR NAME . . .

If you give a witch your name
You know just what she'll do
Once she knows the words to use
She'll put a bind on you
She'll seek you out to fill her pot
Double dee, hubble dee, bubble dee, dine
She'll steal your blood, drip, drip, drop
That's the way of a witch's bind

17

THE CALLING COIN

The instant practice ended, Riley and her prime waited for the others to take off for Clawroot, then they turned and headed for the Yippery.

"I don't see what the big deal is. It's not like we're keeping anyone else from doing cool magic. We just figured it out first," Aracely said, throwing her hands up in exasperation.

The rest of the session hadn't gotten any better. None of the other primes had caught on as quickly as they had, and it seemed that everyone was mad about it. When Riley had said that they weren't coming to the dining hall for cookies, Teddy had answered, "Going off alone again? Big surprise."

He didn't want them around, but he also didn't like that they weren't sticking with the group. There really was no winning.

"It's because it was so easy for us." Lydia followed behind Aracely, plucking stray bits of cotton fluff from her curls. "And a lot of these things are hard for prime packs to master."

"We do seem to be strangely good at group magic," Kenver mused.

"That's not a crime, though, and they're treating us like it is!" Aracely sounded genuinely upset. "It's not fair! Teddy and I used to be friends. He's the only other person I know who can tell a brontosaurus from an apatosaurus!"

"I never thought I'd say this, but I kind of miss how Milo used to bother me all the time," Riley admitted. "And I don't like feeling like he's spying on me."

"For Teddy? No way." Dhonielle shook her head. "He wouldn't do that."

A few months ago, Riley would have agreed with her cousin. Now, she wasn't so sure. "It's his prime," she said. "Teddy's his alpha. And I'm just not sure where I fit anymore."

"I went through this with my sisters," Aracely offered knowledgably. "It's always like this at the beginning. There's, like, an entire year when everyone is all confused. But let me tell you something. The first time someone tells their parents that they can't do something—like the dishes or homework or watch their little sister—because their alpha needs them, they'll spend five whole days in their room with no screen privileges. After that, everything is normal again."

"I think what Aracely is trying to say is that Milo still loves you. He just needs time," Lydia said.

"We all do," Kenver added.

"Isn't that what I just said?" Aracely asked, throwing her hands in the air.

"It is," Riley assured her, smiling in spite of the sad feeling that crept in whenever she thought of Milo. "And thanks. It helps."

They arrived at the Yippery a few moments later. From the outside, it looked exactly as it had the last time Riley had been here: dark and empty. Ter had been keeping the lights off and she'd even been careful not to disturb the old spiderwebs around the front door. Inside, however, the whole place was warm and welcoming, and the air smelled pleasantly of lavender.

"You brought it?" she asked eagerly.

"We brought it." Riley reached into her pocket and produced the coin the boy had given her in La Prima Tazza, dropping it into Ter's open palm.

Everyone leaned in to look. Riley and Dhonielle had updated the others over text, but they hadn't had a chance to see the coin in person yet.

Ter held it out where everyone could see, then turned the coin over, studying the symbols emblazoned on each side, which Riley had inspected the previous night: the river and the letters.

"It's a calling coin," Teralyn explained. "Witches use

them in several ways: to gain entry to a sacred space, to participate in coven works, to prove they even have a coven. But we can also use them to contact someone directly. They all have their own designs, making them unique to the person."

"So it's like a phone number?" Aracely said.

Laughing, Ter retrieved the garden orb from one of the top bunks and set it on the ground in the middle of the room, wrapping a velvety purple scarf around its base to keep it from rolling away.

"Kind of," she said.

She balanced the coin on top of the orb. It looked precarious, like the coin might topple if anyone breathed too hard. But then she raised her hand, whispered a few words, and brought her hand down hard, right on top of the coin. When she pulled her hand away, the coin was in the center of the orb.

"Whoa! What was that?" Kenver crouched next to Ter, their eyes locked on the coin in its new location.

Ter looked a little amused at Kenver's sudden enthusiasm. "Just a part of scry work. It's basic witch magic."

"What's a 'scry'?" Aracely asked, taking a seat on Ter's other side.

"Scrying is one of our three forms of magic. It lets us see something that is far away. Witches use it mostly for communication. We just need something shiny or reflective to make it work. Like an orb." Ter smiled up at Riley, and Riley smiled back, thinking of their conversation from the night she'd brought the orb. "Even one that's been in the garden will work."

"How far away can you see?" Dhonielle asked.

"That depends on a lot of things. At first, we can't see far at all. Mostly, we can only reach the members of our own coven or see into places and mirrors we know really well. But as we practice and get stronger, we can reach farther and farther away."

"Like Japan?" Aracely said hopefully.

"Only very powerful witches can reach across oceans," Ter said. "But I've seen my mom reach a witch in Washington State before."

Riley didn't miss the way Ter's voice caught on the word *mom*, or the shadow of sadness that crossed her features. It hadn't occurred to Riley that if Ter was on the run from her coven, that meant she was also on the run from her family.

"Kind of how we use acoustics," Kenver said, mostly to themselves. "It must be a similar property."

"What are the other kinds of witch magic?" Riley had heard that witches could grant wishes and turn someone into a toad, though both seemed a little far-fetched now that she'd met Ter.

"There are three forms of witch magic: flight, which is pretty self-explanatory; scry work, which we've discussed; and rhythm, which allows us to influence the material world through any kind of rhyme," Ter explained. "We can combine them, of course, but those are the basics."

"Wolves also have three forms: alchemy, acoustics, and lithomancy." Kenver ticked them off on their fingers, their excitement making them uncharacteristically loud. "Is that a coincidence?"

"I don't think so," Dhonielle offered, creeping closer to the group on the floor. "I read once that wolf magic and witch magic evolved separately, but they share roots. Like two limbs of the same tree. So it makes sense that there are three forms of each."

"And that those three forms behave similarly," Kenver added.

"Because all magic is related," Ter finished.

"Maybe we should get this over with?" Lydia was still standing by the front door, her arms crossed over her chest. She looked nervous. "Not that this isn't all extremely interesting, but we really should get you off Wax & Wayne lands sooner rather than later."

"Oh, um, sure," Ter said, her cheeks flushing. "I'm sorry. I didn't mean to drag this out."

"It's okay," Riley said, feeling defensive of Ter, even though Lydia was right. They didn't have time to waste.

Ter cleared her throat and collected the orb in both hands, drawing it toward her as she softly whispered something. The orb filled with a roiling purple smoke.

In the center, the bronze coin began to glow dimly like a sun behind dark clouds.

"Pretty," Aracely murmured, mesmerized by the colors.

Then the cloud faded and was replaced by a face Riley recognized as that of the boy from the coffee shop. He was washed in purple and a little bit see-through, but he was there. She felt a small flutter of victory. It had worked! Ter could talk to the Free Witches, and they would help her untangle the rest of the mess she was in.

The boy smiled and his eyes gleamed dangerously when he said, "There you are, Teralyn."

Ter gasped and staggered away from the orb, pressing her back flat against the wall of the cabin. "No," she muttered in a quiet, terrified voice.

The boy's smile grew, and then so did he. The shape of him rose up out of the orb, growing taller and taller, until it was like he stood with them inside the room. The only reason Riley knew he wasn't actually here was that he was still slightly purple and mostly transparent.

"Stop ignoring your responsibility and come home," he said.

Riley felt her guts give a vicious twist as she understood what had happened. This boy wasn't from the Free Witches at all. He was one of the Flint Witches, the coven Ter had been running from all along. And Riley had led him straight to her.

"No," Ter said, and even though she was trembling, she climbed to her feet and looked the boy straight in the eye. "I won't. You can't make me."

The boy shook his head and sighed heavily. "This will happen, whether you want it to or not. It will be better for everyone, especially your new friends, if you return now."

"She said no," Riley said, stepping between the image of the boy and Ter.

"I'm afraid that doesn't work for me," the boy said, turning his head toward Riley. "Thank you for all your assistance, little pup. I couldn't have done this without you." Then the boy's gaze shifted back to Ter. "You can run away and make no sound," he chanted, "but all that hides will soon be found."

He raised his hand, and a green thread began to extend from his palm. It snaked away from him and out of view—headed, Riley realized with horror, for Ter.

"See you soon, cuz," the boy said.

Riley targeted the orb and began to howl. Instantly, three other calls joined hers—Aracely's, Kenver's, and Dhonielle's—each focused on the globe in the center of the room while Lydia yanked a mattress from one of the beds and threw it on top of the orb.

There was a muffled *BOOM!* as the glass exploded, and the image of the boy vanished from sight.

18

UNBECOMING

"Who was that?" Lydia rose from the now-tattered mattress, where she'd fallen, her eyes ablaze. It was so strange to see Lydia angry that for a second Riley didn't react. "And what kind of spell did he just do?"

"Hey! Don't shout at her!" Riley shifted so that she stood between Lydia and Ter, her boots crunching on little bits of exploded garden orb.

"Um, did you just see the same thing I did?" Lydia said. "A witch just threatened us! And it sounded like he cast a spell that would lead him straight to her. To us!"

"Yeah, that is *not* good," Dhonielle said, wrapping her arms tight around her middle and eyeing the remains of the orb warily.

"I think this has gone far enough." Lydia planted her hands on her hips and looked pointedly at Ter. "We tried. And I was on board with trying. But this is bad news. Either she leaves or I go straight to Great Callahan. We can't keep hiding a witch—*the* witch—here."

Riley swallowed hard. She couldn't tell if she was more upset that Lydia was threatening to go to her mother or that things had suddenly gone so wrong. No, scratch that. She was upset because she'd tried to do something good, and it had turned out she'd been tricked. It made her feel useless and gullible. But in spite of those things, she still believed that nothing good would come of turning Ter over to her mom.

"Don't make threats like some kind of lone wolf. Whatever we do, we'll do it together," Riley said, aware of how everyone was looking to her for assurances. "Because we're a pack, right?"

Lydia's mouth pinched into a frown and she didn't look happy, but after a brief hesitation, she nodded. "We're a pack," she repeated.

Riley cleared her throat. "There has to be some other way to find the Free Witches."

"There's no time for that." Ter's voice was soft. She had crossed the room to sit on her bunk. She looked so small and so tired.

Riley wished she could tell her it would all be okay, but the truth was, Riley had no idea. And sometimes, things weren't okay.

"That was a tracing spell," Ter said. "They work fast. They're probably already on their way here."

"Then there's no time to lose." Lydia spun on her heel and left the cabin, steps aimed for Clawroot.

"Wait!"

Riley vaulted out of the Yippery after Lydia. All she knew was that she had to stop her, so she tugged on the wolf inside her and transformed, racing past Lydia to block her path.

"We have to say something!" said Lydia, skidding to a stop. "She's the Nameless Witch! Or she will be. It's been four days. More than we agreed to. And now the Flint Witches know she's here. We can't keep that a secret!"

Riley met Lydia's eyes and felt that familiar surge of warmth in her cheeks, the delightful dipping in her stomach. Over the summer, those sensations had knocked her off balance, but now they were complicated and strange. She had responsibilities that she hadn't had before.

Riley was Lydia's alpha. She had to focus on that instead of her other feelings.

I know that! I know, Riley said, sending her words into Lydia's mind. *Just, please . . . Just wait a second and let me think.*

Lydia frowned, but she crossed her arms and waited. Lydia was nothing if not patient and thoughtful.

Soon, the others were there, trotting up the path. Dhonielle looked like she was frightened out of her mind. Riley couldn't blame her. In the blink of an eye, this had gone from a simple but important mission to something much more urgent.

Riley paced back and forth across the narrow path, transforming from wolf to girl as she did.

"There has to be a way to help her," Riley said, mostly to herself.

Lydia answered, "There is. We tell your mom."

"We can't tell my mom," Riley said. "You heard her at the emergency forum. She wants to capture the Nameless Witch and imprison or kill her, not help her."

"But we haven't even given her the chance to help," Lydia said. "Maybe she would if she knew Ter like we do."

"I don't think so." Riley felt heavy as she spoke. She thought of what Mama N had told her the night before. That Mama C's parents had been so angry and terrorized by the eighth Nameless Witch that Mama C had grown up fearing all witches. "She really doesn't like witches."

"We don't have any other options, though, do we?" Lydia shook her head and started walking. "We don't even have a clue of what to do."

"I might."

Riley and Lydia froze at the sound of Kenver's voice. They turned to find Kenver a few paces behind, their hands tucked into the pockets of their puffy blue coat.

"A way to help Ter?" Riley asked, not ready to believe her ears.

Kenver's head bobbed up and down. "I was thinking about how wolves sometimes leave the pack. You know. That they can relinquish their wolf if they choose? Many of us might be born with the wolf inside us, but keeping it is a choice. If someone decides they don't want to keep it, then they perform the New Moon Rite—which obviously has to be done at the time of a new moon—and release the wolf back into the world."

That sounded familiar to Riley. It was rare, but she'd heard stories about members of the pack who had decided that they didn't want to be wolves. It wasn't shameful or tragic or anything. It was a choice. She was reminded of Mama C telling her that the ability to choose was one of the most sacred parts of wolf magic. Even if Riley couldn't imagine wanting to unbecome a wolf, it made sense that some people would want a different kind of life.

"You think that would work on a witch?" she asked hopefully.

"I think it could," Kenver said. "And if Ter can unbecome a witch, then surely she can't also *become* the Nameless Witch."

"But she'd have to give up all her magic." Aracely frowned sadly. "She wouldn't be able to fly or any of it. That sounds terrible."

It did sound terrible. Riley wouldn't want to give up her wolf. She couldn't possibly give up her prime pack and the magic they shared. The thought made her throat squeeze tight and her eyes fill with tears.

"Well, if the only other option is to become Nameless,

then it's the better of the two," Dhonielle offered, though she didn't sound like she believed it.

"Hang on," Lydia said. "We don't have any real reason to believe a wolf rite will work on a witch, do we?" She looked to Kenver for the answer.

Kenver scowled in thought. "We don't have any reason to suspect it won't. Dhonielle says that all magic has the same roots, so surely our rites bear similarities to witch spells. It's worth a shot."

Lydia looked skeptical, like she was on the verge of marching straight into Clawroot. Riley knew she could convince her, but she had to act fast.

"We have eight days until the equinox, right? When the spell completes and Ter fully becomes the Nameless Witch," Riley said. And then, without waiting for a reply, she added, "How many days until the new moon?"

This was a risk, because Riley didn't know the answer, and if the number was more than eight, then she had nothing.

"None," Dhonielle said as if in apology. "It starts first thing tomorrow, but like the full moon, the cycle lasts about three days."

Riley couldn't believe their good luck. "Okay, that's good, because we don't know how long it will take the witches to track Ter here. So, how about this? If Ter is willing, we try the New Moon Rite. If it works, then the problem is solved, and Ter can leave anytime she wants.

If it doesn't work, I promise we'll take her to my mom and tell her everything."

"Yep," said Kenver.

"Works for me," sang Aracely.

"Yeah," echoed Dhonielle.

Lydia hesitated before puffing out a sharp breath and shaking her head. "Okay, okay. I'm in."

It felt good to have her pack's support. They hadn't had long to think about any of this, but Riley knew they were doing the right thing. Not only for wolves, but for Ter.

"What if Ter doesn't want to?" Aracely said, interrupting Riley's thoughts. "I mean, *I* wouldn't want to. I'd want to find another way if it were happening to me."

"It kind of did happen to us," Kenver added softly. "And I don't think any of us liked it."

"We didn't like it at all," Riley said, shuddering at the memory of waiting to hear the call of First Wolf. She remembered too well how it had felt to see everyone else running into the woods to transform into wolves for the first time. How it had felt to be left behind. She couldn't imagine giving up her wolf again. How could she ask Ter to give up her magic?

She was still turning the problem this way and that in her mind when footsteps approached from the direction of the Yippery.

All five of them turned toward the sound to see Ter stepping out from the trees a few yards away. She was bundled in her purple cloak, her breath coming out in white puffs, and she looked determined.

"I'm willing," she said, looking just as brave and scared as she had that first night in the woods. "I heard every word. And I want to try the New Moon Rite."

19

FRIENDS

They made their plan right there in the woods. Dhonielle and Kenver were in charge of research, Aracely and Lydia would collect any supplies they might need, and Riley would stay close to Ter for as long as possible.

Before they were done, Ter had returned to the cabin. Riley hurried after her, practicing what she might say in her head, but she didn't really know what to say to someone who was about to make such a huge sacrifice.

When Riley arrived at the cabins, Ter was nowhere to be found. She wasn't on the front porch of the Yippery or inside it. Riley even checked each of the other cabins, but the only things inside them were spiders and a few old candy-bar wrappers.

Telling herself that the witches couldn't have gotten here that fast and they definitely couldn't have made it through the wards without raising the alarm, Riley kept herself from panicking. But just barely.

"Hello?" called Riley, creeping around behind the cabin. "Ter?"

No answer.

"Ter?" she called, louder, and this time she heard a very quiet sniffling in response.

Riley peered into the woods. The sound had been too brief for her to pinpoint a direction.

"I hear you," she called.

Ter sniffled again, and the sound seemed to be coming from everywhere all at once. As though it were bouncing like a reflection in a hall of mirrors.

Riley was just about to pick a direction at random when it occurred to her that if she wanted to find a witch, she really should be looking up. She tipped her head back, and instantly her eyes landed on a flash of purple high in the trees.

"There you are," she called, moving cautiously toward the tree.

"Here I am," Ter said sadly. "Maybe for the last time."

Ter shifted so that Riley could see her clearly as she stepped off a slender branch of the tree and slowly floated down, turning in little circles like a ballerina in a music box. She landed in front of Riley with tear-stained cheeks and eyes red from crying.

"Sorry," she said. "I know you don't want me out here where people can see. It's just the most perfect feeling in the world, you know?"

"I do," Riley answered immediately, then realized that she didn't know how it felt to fly. "I mean, that's how I feel about shifting into my wolf form. It makes me feel . . ." Riley searched for the right word, then at the same second she and Ter both said, "Connected."

They smiled. For a moment, it felt like they were just two people becoming friends.

"I just wanted to, um, to feel that as much as possible before . . . before . . ." Ter shook her head, unable to finish the sentence, and Riley realized that if the New Moon Rite worked, then after tomorrow morning, Ter would never be able to fly again.

It didn't seem fair that something so terrible could happen to someone who had done nothing to deserve it. Ter hadn't asked to become the next Nameless Witch, just like Riley and the others hadn't asked to be connected to the Devouring Wolf last summer. In both cases, it was the result of something someone else had done a long time ago.

And Ter was going to have to fundamentally change who she was to avoid an even worse fate. That was *definitely* not fair.

Riley took a small step closer to Ter. "I wish we could find another solution."

"Me too," Ter said. Tears were spilling down her cheeks when she added, "I really love being a witch."

Instinct took over, and Riley wrapped her arms around

Ter, pulling her into a tight hug. "I'm so sorry, Ter," Riley said, realizing that she was crying, too.

For a few minutes, they stayed that way. Then, with a deep breath, Ter pulled away.

"Is there anything I can do to help?" Riley asked. "What do you need?"

Ter laughed a little and rubbed the tears from her eyes. "It means a lot that you care enough to ask."

Anger flared in Riley all over again.

"Don't take this the wrong way, but your parents must really suck," Riley said, frowning.

To Riley's surprise, Ter shook her head. "No, they don't. It's an honor to be chosen. At least, that's what they say, and maybe it used to be true. The Nameless Witches are the reason witches have been safe for centuries. Most of us wouldn't be here if not for their sacrifice. It's important, I know that. I just wanted my life to be . . . mine."

"You should have a choice," Riley said. "All the Nameless Witches should have had a choice."

"The magic of the Nameless Witch is about choice," Ter answered sadly. "The Nameless Witch sacrifices her own so that all other witches can choose when they come into their power. It's for the good of the many."

Riley thought about First Wolf and how she had worked with a witch to create a similar spell for wolves. Long, long ago, all werewolves were forced to transform on the three nights of the full moon. They weren't in control of their own magic, their own bodies, and every full moon they were forced to shift into wolves regardless of where they were or who they were with. But First Wolf changed that by ensuring that only a wolf's first transformation would be triggered by the moon. After that, each wolf could control when they changed or if they changed at all.

It was all about choice and safety.

"If I were a better person, I'd be happy to make this sacrifice," Ter said.

"I don't think wanting to live your own life makes you a bad person," Riley said.

"Selfish, then. That's what my mom said. That my reaction was selfish. And all the Nameless Witches before me would be ashamed." Ter heaved a sigh. "She's probably right."

"You don't know that. Maybe some of the others didn't want to become nameless either. Maybe they'd think what you're doing is brave."

"Scared is more like it."

"My mom says that you can't be brave unless you're also really scared. Otherwise, you're just being bold." Riley had never completely understood Mama N's words before. "Making a decision that goes against what so many people want from you is brave. And sometimes, it's necessary."

Tears reappeared in the young witch's eyes. She reached for Riley's hands. "But what if—what if the magic is so much a part of me that I change anyway? What if I'm different no matter what?"

Riley squeezed Ter's cold fingers, trying to warm them up. This, at least, was something Riley did know about.

"It's okay to change. We change a little bit every day, some days more than others." Riley raised their linked hands. "Just look at *us*. A few days ago, we never would have been friends, because I believed wolves and witches were natural enemies. You changed that."

"Friends?" Ter said hopefully. "We're friends?"

Riley hadn't realized it until she'd said it out loud, but sometimes the truth snuck up on you like that. "Friends," she confirmed.

"Then can I share something with you, before it's too late?" Ter asked.

"O-kay . . ." Riley said, drawing the word out so it almost became a question.

"It's not bad," Ter promised. "Well, unless you're afraid of heights. Are you?" Riley shook her head, and Ter beamed. "Good. Hold on tight."

Before Riley could ask what Ter meant, she felt the soles of her boots leave the ground. Little by little, they rose into the air, up past the bushes and sapling trees that grew above Riley's head, up past tree branches and old squirrel nests, up, up, up, until they crested over the treetops, where the air was wintery and cold.

"This is amazing," Riley said, breathless, as she looked out over the hills and valleys of Wax & Wayne, and far into the distance, where the tallest buildings of the university stood atop the hill. Their little flags waved blue and red against the white clouds. "Please don't drop me."

"I promise I won't," Ter said.

And as they flew, Riley thought she saw flashes of early pink blossoms in the winter wood. It was a perfect moment in an imperfect day.

IF YOU GIVE A WITCH YOUR NAME . . .

If you give a witch your name
You know just what she'll do
Once she knows the words to use
She'll scry to find you
She'll find you with her mirror ball
Double dee, hubble dee, bubble dee, bry
She'll find your secrets and you'll tell all
That's the way of a witch's scry

20

A FEW NEW GROUND RULES

It was sheer luck that the next day was Saturday and as of Monday, it would be spring break. At least they wouldn't have to worry about school on top of everything else.

But just as Riley was putting on her shoes and discreetly slipping packs of crackers and beef jerky into a bag for Ter, Mama C called a family meeting in the living room.

Riley settled on the arm of their overstuffed sofa and tried not to look like she was ready to bolt out the front door, when that was exactly what she was ready to do.

Darcy dropped onto the sofa next to Riley, and Milo sprawled out on the opposite end, throwing his legs over Darcy's. Mama N was the last to arrive, twisting her hair into a topknot, which meant she was getting ready for yoga.

Mama C had her long, dark hair pulled back in a tight braid, and she was wearing a grim expression. "You all remember what we learned about the new Nameless Witch? Well, the equinox will be here in one week, and usually that wouldn't be worrisome, but"—she paused, eyes flicking to Mama N, who nodded, encouraging her to continue—"there are more witches in town than usual. And that is cause for concern."

"In Lawrence? Why?" Darcy asked.

"We don't know for sure, but we suspect it means they've tracked the Nameless Witch here."

Milo sat up, head turning toward Riley. She avoided making eye contact, which was easy to do when it felt like her stomach was falling through the floor.

Mama N stepped up next to Mama C, a united front, except that while Mama C was nearly glowering, Mama N was smiling as though everything were fine. She said, "Since it's the start of spring break and the three of you won't be in school, we need to put down a few additional ground rules."

"What kind of ground rules?" Darcy narrowed her eyes suspiciously.

"For starters, a curfew." Mama N's chipper voice was at odds with the horrible news she was delivering. "Everyone needs to be home by eight, no exceptions."

"That's so early!" Darcy so rarely got upset with their parents that even a moderate rise in her voice sounded extreme. "I'm seventeen!"

"Which means you're mature enough to handle a

curfew for a few days. We also need a check-in every time you decide to change locations," she added. "So if you're at Wax & Wayne and decide to go home, we expect a phone call. If you're at a friend's house and you decide to go out for coffee, phone call. Tracking stays on at all times."

All three siblings groaned in unison.

"Believe me, it's no picnic for us either. I'm going to have to set up a whole spreadsheet just to keep track of you three," Mama N said, with an amused shake of her head. "And again, only until the equinox passes. After that, we'll reassess."

"We'll be talking with other parents as well," Mama C added. "Just to keep you all as safe as possible. Remember, this isn't anything you've done wrong. It's just the way things need to be right now."

It felt like a punishment to Riley. Though that might have something to do with the fact that she knew exactly who the next Nameless Witch was. And where to find her.

When it seemed like her moms were finished, Riley raised her hand. "May I go to Wax & Wayne, please?" she asked. "Uncle Will and Dhonielle are already on their way. We made these plans before I knew I would need to ask permission."

"Sure," Mama C said with a tight nod. "But no shifting unless you're inside the wards. Understood?"

"Understood." Riley hopped up, kissed her moms on the cheeks, and bounded through the front door before they could change their minds.

"Hold it right there!"

It was Milo, suddenly right behind her.

"What?" Riley said. "Who even says that?"

"Lots of people." Milo crossed his arms over his chest, undeterred. "She's still at the cabin, isn't she? She hasn't left like you said she would."

"Shhh!" Riley grabbed Milo's arm and tugged him away from the house. "I thought you said you would keep my secret?"

"I did!" Milo tugged his arm away. "But it's been longer than you said now, and there are more witches in town, and our moms are worried, and I have a really strong feeling that you shouldn't be keeping this secret anymore."

Riley glanced back at the house, making sure no one else had come out. The front door was closed, but it wouldn't take Darcy long to find the car keys.

"Why are you still hiding her?" Milo demanded. "She's dangerous!"

"I know, but she needs our help. None of this is her fault! It isn't *fair*!"

"Great moons, Riley!" Milo reached up with both hands to grab his hair, tugging at it like his brain was exploding. Which maybe it was. "What are you thinking? We have to tell Mom. *You* have to tell Mom. Do you realize that you are directly disobeying her right now? You're doing exactly what she's asked every wolf in our entire pack *not* to do?"

Riley's stomach pitched violently at the thought. She did know that and thinking about it made her want to vomit because when her mom found out, she was going to be in more trouble than she'd ever been in before. There was a big difference between hiding a bad grade and hiding a witch.

"I know, but Ter doesn't deserve to be locked up against her will. She's just a kid. Like us. Doesn't she deserve a chance to not be the Nameless Witch?" Riley could see the skepticism in her brother's expression. "We think we have a solution. We just need one more day. Please, just keep the secret for one more day."

Milo glanced at the house, then back to his sister. His dark curls flopped into his eyes, just like always, but Riley could feel that new distance between them, stretching out long like a field of wheat. "You're asking me for special treatment," he said.

That hit Riley right in the gut. She was sure that Milo never would have thought that if not for Teddy. And it stung that he was taking Teddy's side over hers.

"No, I'm asking you to trust me because you're my brother and I'm your sister."

At that moment, Uncle Will's van turned up the

driveway and Dhonielle opened the sliding door. "Ready, Riley?"

"Just a sec!" called Riley, then fixed her attention back on her brother. "Trust me for one more day?"

Milo winced, struggling with the decision.

"Please," Riley added.

For a second, she was convinced that he would say no. Then he released a long breath and nodded. "One more day," he said.

"Thank you," Riley sighed, giving him a quick squeeze before jogging over to the van.

"Sure," he grumbled.

As they pulled away from the house, Riley couldn't help but watch her brother growing farther and farther away.

MORE WITCHES
IN THE WOODS

Riley had never given much thought to the New Moon Rite. Mostly because she had never considered unbecoming a wolf. Kenver and Dhonielle had quickly discovered that, like the Full Moon Rite, the New Moon Rite was best performed when the moon was in the sky. Whereas the full moon was high at night, the new moon was high in the morning hours. It was an odd time for a magic spell, but given the tracking spell Ter's cousin had cast, they were all glad to be trying the rite sooner rather than later.

The plan for the ritual was simple. Aracely and Lydia would bring the supplies, Kenver would bring the spell, and they would all meet at the Yippery, then find a good spot for the rite.

But as Riley and Dhonielle followed Uncle Will across the wards of Wax & Wayne, the air shimmered violently purple and green, and the cuffs around their wrists seemed to squeeze. It happened again, and then a third time, as though someone was knocking at the wards.

"Stand back." Uncle Will's voice had dropped dangerously low. He ushered the two of them farther past the wards as he scanned the path they'd just traversed. "Someone is here."

Just then, three figures appeared. They came gliding between the trees like birds, with their bodies tipped forward and their arms held out behind them like wings. If they hadn't been flying, Riley wouldn't have known them for witches.

One was a young man with a shock of blond hair, who was wearing a leather jacket. Another was short, with pale brown skin and twists of black curls haloed around her head. She was dressed in jeans and a black wool jacket, with a fuchsia infinity scarf wrapped around her neck. The third one was also short, with olive skin and graying chestnut waves. She wore a rainbow cardigan that flowed over green pants—and, okay, that one Riley would have pegged as a witch. Even without the flying.

They landed lightly and walked the rest of the way, stopping before they reached the wards. That was when Riley realized that the young man was the boy she and Dhonielle had met in the coffee shop. The one who had appeared in Ter's orb and demanded that she come home. Ter's cousin.

Riley's first instinct was to hide, but it was too late for that. The boy's eyes found her and Dhonielle. He smiled a sneery smile of recognition, then raised a gloved hand to waggle his fingers at them.

A low growl started in Uncle Will's throat, but the three witches seemed unbothered.

The one in the rainbow cardigan stepped forward. She smiled, holding her hands up as if to show she was unarmed. Which was ridiculous, because witches were always armed. Just not with physical weapons.

"My apologies for the intrusion," she said. "My name is Robin Mercy."

Mercy. Riley took a harder look at this witch and realized that she'd seen her before, too. Except she hadn't really seen her, because she'd been cast in shadow. Robin Mercy was one of the witches who had come to her house that night. She was the one who had spotted Riley on the stairs.

"I am here on behalf of the Free Witches of Lawrence," she said pleasantly.

Riley caught Dhonielle's eye and knew they were thinking the same thing.

"*He's* not!" Riley pointed at the boy.

"Hello again, pups," the boy said, with that same sneer of a smile.

"You shouldn't be here," Uncle Will said. Riley noted that his fingers had curled into fists and that every muscle in his body was rigid. Ready to fight.

"That is absolutely right. We shouldn't be here and, believe me, if I had any other choice, we wouldn't be." Somehow, Robin Mercy's voice managed to be both warm and cheerful in spite of Uncle Will's hostility. "But I'm afraid there is a matter of great concern that I must bring to your attention."

"Whatever it is, say it and leave," Uncle Will ground out.

"Use small words, Robin," the boy said. "We want to make sure he understands."

"Excuse you?" Dhonielle stepped in front of her dad, uncharacteristically bold. "Take it back."

Robin's hand went up instantly. "Darren, please. That's not how we handle things here."

"So I've heard," Darren muttered, with a sideways glare at the rainbow-clad woman. "Which is why we have this problem to begin with. The wolves out west know better than to disrespect witches so plainly."

"Respect is a journey," Dhonielle said sharply.

"And you haven't even left the porch," Riley added.

Darren's lip curled as he glared at Dhonielle. "Do you know what wolf blood is good for, young pup?"

Uncle Will stepped in front of them again.

"Hear me now, my dear, sweet Darren. These words you speak aren't meant for sharin'," said the third woman.

Darren's eyes widened, and he opened his mouth, but

nothing came out. Riley had to stifle a laugh. The boy had been silenced by a spell.

"Again, my apologies. We mean no offense. Please, let me introduce my covenmate Justina Welsh," said Robin, gesturing to the Black woman. Then she nodded toward the boy. "And this is Darren Grimsley, a representative of the Flint Witch Coven of Salina."

I can't believe he's related to Ter! Dhonielle spoke softly into Riley's mind.

Seems like she doesn't get a lot of support from her family, Riley answered, studying the boy more closely. Apart from the blond hair, it was hard to find any similarities between the witch she'd come to care about and the boy in front of her.

Poor Ter, Dhonielle murmured. *I'm glad you're* my *cousin.*

"I don't care who you are," Uncle Will said. "Whatever it is you have to say, say it and go."

Robin's smile faltered. "I'm afraid that it has come to our attention that there is a young witch inside your wards, and we must have her back."

"We have no witches here," Uncle Will said, turning to leave.

"But you do," Robin insisted. Her gaze shifted to Riley so suddenly that Riley felt her heart jump in her chest. "I wish it weren't the case, but we have compelling evidence."

Riley swallowed hard, trying to convince her body not

to react and give her away. Darren still couldn't speak, or she was certain he'd have had no trouble telling Uncle Will that she and Dhonielle knew more than they were saying. For some reason, though, Robin Mercy wasn't revealing what she knew.

Robin looked back to Uncle Will. "She may be hiding or hurt. Whatever the case, we request that you return her to us with haste, or I'm afraid we'll have to revisit this matter under . . . different circumstances."

Uncle Will stilled at that, seeming to understand something that hadn't been spoken aloud. After a long minute, he nodded. "I'll take it to the greats. If there's a witch here, we'll find her and return her to you."

Robin clasped her hands together. "That is exactly what I hoped you'd say."

"We can give you twenty-four hours," Justina said, with a sideways glance at Darren. "Then we'll be back."

The three witches turned and rose into the air, gliding through the trees the way they'd come. Riley's heart was hammering in her chest, her mind a jumble of thoughts, so it took her a moment to understand that Uncle Will was speaking to them.

"We'll be fine," Dhonielle was saying. "Promise."

Uncle Will pulled them both into a crushing hug, his muscled arms easily encompassing the two of them at once. "I'll be back. Just stay inside the wards. They won't cross them, if they know what's good for them," he said.

Before Riley had fully processed what was happening, Uncle Will was gone.

"What?" she said, turning to Dhonielle.

"He's going to gather the greats. Share the message and probably start combing the woods for Ter," she said as though this were something Riley should know. "Because things weren't bad enough already."

"Right." In another hour, Wax & Wayne would be crawling with wolves. Including her moms. And with that many wolves searching for a single witch, it wouldn't be long before she was found.

"Riley?" Dhonielle waved a hand in front of her face. "Why do you think Robin didn't say anything? It was obvious that she knows we know about Ter. She could have just said it."

Riley blinked as her cousin came into focus once more. Why *hadn't* Robin turned them in? "I think she was giving us time," she said.

"For what?"

"To help Ter," Riley said, and for some reason, she knew it was true even though she'd only ever seen Robin Mercy once before. "I don't think they like the Flint Witches very much. They definitely don't like Darren Grimsley."

"Okay, so what now?" Dhonielle asked.

Riley peered up between bare branches to the bright blue sky beyond. Somewhere up there was the new moon, ready and waiting for them to perform the rite. Justina had promised them twenty-four hours before the witches came back. They still had time. They could still help Ter unbecome the Nameless Witch.

Riley smiled and turned her steps toward Tenderfoot Camp. "We stick to the plan," she said.

22

HOW TO UNWITCH A WITCH

Thirty minutes later, they were seated with Ter on the narrow front porch of the Yippery, telling her about what had just happened.

"The tricky part of a tracer spell is getting it to track the right person or thing," she explained. "Once Darren had a lead on me through that scry, it was probably a piece of cake." Her shoulders slumped. "But if he's working with the Free Witches, I guess they won't help me."

"I'm not so sure about that," Riley said. "They don't seem to like him very much."

"Yeah, one of them put a spell on him so that he couldn't talk!" Dhonielle snickered.

"I bet he didn't like that very much." Ter smiled conspiratorially. "He hates when people are stronger than he is."

"Is that why he's so mean?" Riley asked.

"Oh, he's not—" Ter stopped herself. "I mean, he wasn't always like this. He just really thinks I should be happy to become the Nameless Witch. He says all the same things everyone else does. That it's an honor, and blah blah blah. I think he thinks it makes our family special or something."

"Then *he* should do it," Riley said, suddenly angry.

"It doesn't work like that."

"How does it work?" Riley asked. "How does everyone know that you're next?"

"She told me." Ter smiled at the memory. "It was lovely. When the spell started, I didn't know what was going on, but then I was wrapped in a cocoon of rainbows, and there she was, the Nameless Witch. She told me that the magic had chosen me and that when she passed on the equinox, I'd take her place. I told her that I was honored but that I didn't want to do it, and she said that it was too late. The spell had a life of its own."

"What do you think will happen to the spell after we unwitch you?" Dhonielle asked. "Will that stop the spell? Or will it be forced to find another witch?"

"I don't know," Ter admitted.

"Got the rite," Kenver said, jogging around the cabin and scaring Dhonielle nearly out of her skin.

"Oh, no, no, no," Dhonielle muttered, her shoulders hunched up to her ears. "You can't go sneaking around like that."

"Sorry, I thought we were supposed to be sneaky."

"Hey, hey! I've got the goooooods!" Aracely's voice

ranged out over the empty campground, startling all three of them. "I've got silence stones and a candle, and this little plastic moon, because I thought we should have something that looked like the moon, since it's, ya know, daytime and it's called the New *Moon* Rite. I also brought some candy. Anybody want a gummy peach?"

Dhonielle spun around, wide-eyed. "Shhh! Keep your voice down. Remember the part where this is a whole big secret?"

"It's not like anyone comes out here at this time of year," Aracely said, but she spoke more quietly.

"Usually, that's true, but in about half an hour there will be a lot of wolves out searching for Ter, so we need to work fast," Riley said, giving Kenver and Aracely the quickest possible rundown of all that had happened this morning.

"Where's Lyd—I mean, where's Blondie?" Dhonielle asked Aracely, remembering at the last second not to use Lydia's name in front of Ter, who would hopefully not be the next Nameless Witch by the time they were through. "I thought she was supposed to be with you."

"She didn't show up, and I was just a teensy bit late, so I thought maybe she'd gone ahead and I should just go, but she's not here either?"

"We haven't seen her," Dhonielle said. "Maybe her uncles wouldn't let her out of the house so early?"

"They usually get up before dawn to start making treats

for the Sweet Tooth," Riley said. "She wasn't expecting to have any trouble getting out of the house."

"Do you think something's wrong?" Dhonielle asked.

Riley closed her eyes and focused on the threads of energy that connected her to the rest of her prime. *Lydia?* she called. But there was no answer.

There could be any number of reasons for her absence—Riley knew that—but she couldn't help worrying that Lydia had changed her mind and decided not to come. The thought made Riley uncomfortable. She wanted her prime to work together, to be together even if things were hard. For one of their five to be missing felt like something was off. Wrong. And what they were about to do was too important for things to feel wrong from the start.

She opened her eyes again. "We'll have to look for her later. We have a spell to do and not much time to do it in."

"Ah, about that," Kenver started. "The good news is that this rite is pretty simple," said Kenver, like it wasn't good news at all.

"Is there bad news?" Riley asked.

"Yeah . . ." Kenver dragged the word out and avoided looking Ter in the eye. "The bad news is that the rite can only be performed if the prime pack is there to receive the released wolf. Or witch, in this case. And as far as I know, you don't have one."

"She has us," Riley said. "Do you think that will work?"

Kenver hesitated, then said, "It might."

"But . . . she's not a wolf." Dhonielle shifted uncomfortably. "We can't be her coven."

"Yeah, I don't want to be a witch," said Aracely. "I mean, is that what would happen? Would we receive her witch magic?"

Riley looked from her cousin to Kenver to Aracely, sensing their reluctance. She didn't have the answers, but she knew they still had to try.

"You said that wolf and witch magics are two limbs of the same tree, right?" Riley aimed her question at her cousin. "But they split off from each other a long time ago? Don't you think that means that we can share magic like this?"

Dhonielle frowned, but Kenver was nodding. "That does make sense. There's no reason a witch's magic should hurt us. Or any reason we would become witches ourselves."

"Wasn't it a witch who helped First Wolf cast that big spell so we weren't tied to the full moon in the first place?" Aracely asked. "Seems like we were meant to work together, if you think about it."

Everyone stared at Aracely.

It was Ter who spoke first.

"Her name was Honor Finch," she said. "The witches have a story about her. It's not a good one. At least not the version that I've heard. They call her a traitor, because she's the reason that the wolves learned how to take full control of their magic. And the wolves were ungrateful and eventually turned on the witches."

"That's not true! Witches turned on wolves!" shouted Aracely.

"I'm not saying it's true." Ter flushed, her cheeks turning bright pink. "Or I didn't mean to. I only meant to say that her name was Honor, and maybe you're right. Wolves and witches aren't as different as we think."

"Maybe not," Riley said. "And we—Ter—doesn't have much time. Is everyone willing to try?"

Kenver nodded instantly. Aracely was next, then Dhonielle. Then, suddenly, Lydia was there, too.

"Hey," she huffed, out of breath.

"Oh, thank goodness!" Aracely clapped her hands together. "I thought you'd bolted on us," she admitted, without any hint of malice. Just pure, loud honesty.

Lydia wrapped an arm around Aracely's shoulders. "I would never bolt on my prime. But I do have bad news. We can't do the rite. At least not here."

"Why?" Riley asked.

"Because the reason I was late is that there are approximately ten million wolves out here today. And if we don't get out of Wax & Wayne fast, they're going to find us before we can so much as light a magic candle."

23

THE NEW MOON RITE

There were not ten million wolves on the grounds of Wax & Wayne, but the number didn't seem too far off.

Riley took the lead and aimed away from Clawroot. This seemed like the best direction, especially if Great Callahan had called any sort of meeting to discuss the Free Witches' ultimatum. The hardest part was keeping Ter hidden. A pack of wolves wasn't going to raise any alarms, but a strange girl in a purple cloak roaming around while everyone was on the lookout for a young witch most definitely was.

Dhonielle and Kenver shifted into wolves and traveled ahead of the rest, their senses alert for trouble, while Lydia and Aracely did the same behind, wary of anyone who might have picked up the scent of a mostly human girl and could be on their trail.

Riley and Ter raced, hand in hand, through the wintery

woods until they'd passed through the wards and were safely on the other side.

When Riley felt they'd gone far enough, she stopped in a clearing and called everyone back.

"Okay," Riley said, still breathing hard from the run. "Let's do this. Quick."

The wolves would be searching for the witch inside the wards, which would give them a little more time to do the ritual. But being on the outside of them meant they didn't have any protection other than the silence stones Aracely had brought with her. Someone would have to be very close by to overhear them.

"We need you in the center," Kenver said, pulling Ter into the middle as Aracely set the silence stones around their circle, then lit the candle and handed it to Ter. "And, well, if you were a wolf, you would call to us, but since you're not, maybe you can . . . offer your magic with a rhyme?"

Ter nodded confidently, but Riley could hear the tremble in her voice when she answered, "I can do that."

"Okay," said Kenver, then took their spot in the circle. "Then this will be a lot like the Summoning Rite we tried this summer. We'll create a calling circle for protection, but Ter is going to be returning the call. Or, in this case, releasing her magic with a rhythm spell."

In spite of the cold, sweat prickled in Riley's palms.

This was their only shot, and they all knew it. "Are you ready, Ter?"

Ter held the candle tightly. "I am, but first, I wanted to say thank you. I know this is a lot to ask and you don't have any reason to trust witches, and I'm really grateful. Especially to you, Riley."

Riley nearly gasped. "How did you learn my name?"

"Your mom said it."

Riley frowned, trying to recall when Ter had been around either of her moms.

Ter continued, "When we were talking over scry the other night."

Mama N! She had called Riley's name just before coming into her bedroom that night.

"You've known my real name for days," Riley said.

Ter nodded. "And after this, I hope to learn all of your names."

"We'll be happy to share them with you," Lydia assured her.

Ter smiled warmly at each of them. "Okay," she said. "Now I'm ready."

Riley stood so that she could see Ter's face. Then she and the others began to call. Their voices wove together, soft tones creating a harmonious ring around Ter. Magic stirred between them, humming pleasantly against their skin, tickling their tongues.

For a second, Ter stood with her eyes closed, letting the sensation wash over her. Then she opened her eyes and spoke her rhyme.

"This magic that has graced my veins, I give it to the world again."

It came out as barely a whisper, as though she weren't ready to release it.

"This magic that has graced my veins, I give it to the world again."

It was louder this time, her voice gaining substance and competing with the sound of the wolves' call.

"This magic that has graced my veins, I give it to the world again."

This time, she was nearly shouting. Her voice rose high, spiraling toward the sky. She repeated the rhyme, again and again, until a glow began somewhere inside her chest. It was bright and pale, like a star, with spears of rainbow colors that flickered.

It was working. The rite was unmaking Ter's magic, and she would be free. Of her coven, and of the magic they'd forced upon her.

Riley felt a swell of relief, and also sadness for all that Ter was giving up. But she was proud of her for refusing to let other people define her. Riley raised her voice along with the others.

Ter stopped speaking, her eyes going wide, wide, wide,

as the glowing in her chest grew. She looked at Riley in shock, and then the light exploded outward, throwing Riley onto her back.

Riley heard a scream.

Then there was nothing.

24

THE NEW MOON WRONG?

When Riley opened her eyes again, the sky was swirling, and the trees seemed to be spinning around and around, interspersed with strange flashes of light.

Squeezing her eyes shut, Riley rolled onto her stomach and tried to get onto her hands and knees. The movement made everything spin more violently, and she thought she might vomit. Then, slowly, the world began to settle itself once more. The trees stopped their circling motion, and the ground seemed stable enough to hold her.

Someone else was on the ground just a few yards away.

"Dho—Kitty?" called Riley, squinting as she rose to her feet. "Blondie?"

Riley blinked and saw that all five of the prime pack had been flung onto their backs and were now struggling to their feet again. In the middle, standing exactly where she'd been before, was Ter.

Her eyes were closed, and she still held the candle, its

flame flickering before her. The light that had appeared in her chest during the rite was gone, but now she was cocooned in a soft glow.

"She looks like the moon," murmured Riley.

"Did it work?" Lydia asked.

"Did *what* work?" Great Callahan's voice boomed ahead of her as she strode into the clearing.

The shock Riley felt in that moment was nothing compared to what she felt in the next when another figure appeared behind her mom.

"Milo!" cried Riley, too shocked to remember not to use his name.

Milo didn't answer. Next to him stood Teddy Griffin, a look of triumph on his face. The rest of their prime came along behind them and so did Bethany Books, with her big blue glasses and sandaled feet.

Riley couldn't look at Milo any longer. It was clear what had happened. He'd chosen his pack over her, and his pack had turned them in.

"Nobody move," Great Callahan said, then turned to Riley. "You, come here." Without waiting for an answer, Great Callahan walked away from the group, expecting Riley to follow. Which was exactly what Riley did.

Dread filled her belly, making it hard to put one foot in front of the other, but it wasn't the impending conversation with her mom that weighed her down. It was Milo. The betrayal stung.

"Riley Callahan." Great Callahan's voice was low and cutting. "What on earth were you thinking? Hiding a witch? And . . ." She glanced over to where Ter stood, with her eyes still closed, that strange light glowing around her. "What have you done?"

It was too late for anything but the truth. "A rite. To release Ter's witch."

Mama C's jaw clenched. Her gaze shifted to the trees overhead, and she glared. Hard.

Riley didn't think she'd ever seen her mom this mad. It made her look different. Scary.

"Ter" was all she said.

Riley nodded. "Her name is Teralyn Grimsley, and she was selected as the next Nameless Witch. Except she didn't—"

"That is enough!" her mom barked. Riley felt the words shoot through her like a bolt of ice, freezing her from her head all the way down to her toes. Her mom's expression changed. She was no longer scowling at Riley but looking at her as though in pain. "There are consequences for acting against the pack. I cannot ignore them simply because you're my child. But we'll discuss that later."

Riley had known that there would be consequences if they were caught. She'd assumed they would be the usual brand of punishments. They'd be grounded or assigned to muck the stables for the rest of their lives, or maybe they wouldn't be allowed back to Wax &

Wayne for a time. But the way her mom had said "consequences" just now gave Riley a very bad feeling.

Wolves who broke pack rules received harsh punishments. Sometimes, they had to make a public statement of apology. Sometimes, they were exiled. Surely *that* wasn't was Mama C meant?

"Everyone, get back to Clawroot now. I want the five of you in the Hall of Ancestors. Bethany, help me with the witch."

There wasn't much to say after that.

Mama C ushered everyone into Clawroot with such urgency that Riley barely had time to register that they were bringing a witch inside their most protected site. There were people and wolves everywhere. Somehow, word had spread that the witch had been found, and they were returning to Clawroot to see for themselves.

But they weren't only looking at the witch, carried in Bethany's surprisingly strong arms, with her eyes sealed shut and her hands still clasped around the candle. They were looking at Riley. Did they know? Riley felt her cheeks burning under the scrutiny. If they didn't know yet, they would soon. Everyone would know that she'd broken the pack's rules. Everyone would know that she'd let a witch stay on wolf land.

Riley spent the journey thinking about what she would say when her mother demanded an explanation. She didn't think the truth would take her very far, but maybe it would at least let her shield the rest of her prime. She was the alpha. She would bear the brunt of whatever punishment was headed her way.

Mama C let them into the Hall of Ancestors in the very center of Clawroot. Milo and his pack were told to wait outside while the rest of them went inside the great hall.

The Hall of Ancestors was exactly that: a long hall with high ceilings and walls that had been inscribed with the history of their pack. Carvings of wolves tumbled from one end of the room to the next, their names set into the whorls of their fur in glittering tracks of lithodust, which glowed and twinkled like distant stars. At the farthest end of the hall was a massive fireplace, where a roaring fire had been lit to beat back the chill of winter.

"Sit." Her mother's voice allowed no argument.

Riley and the others did as instructed, and they watched as the adults settled Ter on the floor nearby. Though her eyes were still closed, she wasn't asleep, and she didn't lie down. She just stood there exactly as she had during the rite, the candle burning between her palms.

"Mom," Riley started, hoping to explain herself at least a little, but her mom cut her off with a stern look.

"Not right now."

"Is she okay?" Dhonielle asked, eyes on Ter. "I think she screamed at the end of the rite."

Bethany took a seat at the table and folded her hands on top. "What rite was that?"

"The New Moon Rite," Riley answered, before anyone else could. She could feel her mother's glare, but she kept her eyes on Bethany. "It was my idea. I thought we could use it to remove Ter's magic."

"I see," Bethany said. "Why were you trying to remove her magic?"

"Because"—Riley cast a nervous glance at her mom— "she doesn't want to become the Nameless Witch."

Great Callahan rounded on her daughter. "You've been hiding her this entire time?"

Dhonielle flinched. Aracely's jaw dropped. Lydia and Kenver didn't breathe.

Riley felt like her legs had turned to jelly and melted into the chair.

"I have never known you to be this irresponsible. What were you thinking? Or did that witch put a spell on you?" Her mother caught her by the chin and stared into her eyes, the bone talisman swinging in the air between them. "We should call those witches right now and make them fix whatever it is she's done to you."

"Mom, stop!" Riley sprang to her feet. "She didn't put a spell on me, and we can't give her back to them! Not until we know if it worked."

"It wasn't a bad idea." Bethany's voice was tentative, as if she was just as intimidated by Great Callahan as everyone else. "There are more than a few links between wolf and witch magic, so it's possible that a wolf rite would have a similar effect on a witch. Oh! Especially given what we know—or suspect, rather—about First Wolf's spell. You know, there are some people who think that the witch—"

Great Callahan cut her off with a sharp look. "Stay on topic. What are you saying exactly?"

Bethany cleared her throat. "Right. I'm saying that if they were trying to divorce this young witch from her magic with the New Moon Rite, there's a decent chance it worked. Or is working."

"If she were a *wolf*, what would be happening now?" Riley asked, encouraged.

Bethany's lips pinched together, and she cast a questioning look at Great Callahan, silently asking permission before she answered. Great Callahan nodded, and Bethany continued.

"She would be awake by now. Perhaps in a bit of pain, but the magic would have left her. Which hers clearly hasn't."

"What if she doesn't wake up?" Riley asked, panicked.

No one answered her right away. Which was how Riley knew that her panic was a completely appropriate response. If Ter didn't wake before their twenty-four hours were up, Great Callahan would have to explain to the witches why they didn't have their runaway, when the witches knew that Riley had been hiding her. Or maybe she would simply hand Ter over like this, and then Riley would never know what happened to her.

Each possibility felt worse than the previous one. Riley was almost glad when Uncle Will burst through the massive double doors like a tornado. His eyes flicked across the scene, taking in everything at once.

"It's true?" He growled the question at Mama C, striding into the room with powerful steps. Behind him came Dhonielle's mom and Mama N. "You brought the witch inside Clawroot. When the Flint Witches are itching for a fight? When we've called every wolf in the Hackberry Hill Alliance here to search for her?"

"I'm aware of the circumstances we're in, William." Mama C stood tall, meeting Uncle Will's eyes.

"Then why are you doing this?" Aunt Alexis asked. "We don't mess with witches. Callahans don't mess with witches. Ever."

"I'm certain she has her reasons," Mama N said, moving gracefully around Alexis and Will into the room to stand with Mama C.

"I'd like to know them," Uncle Will said. Riley had rarely seen him angry.

"Our children had something to do with it," Mama C said.

That pulled Uncle Will up short. A little of the anger slipped from his face, and he turned to Dhonielle and then Riley. Understanding seemed to hit him all at once.

"You knew where the witch was all along," he said. "Of course you did."

"Her name is Ter." Riley raised a hand and gestured toward the girl still standing in the center of the room. "We were trying to help her."

"Help her how?" Mama N asked gently.

"From turning into something she didn't want to become," Lydia explained.

"Yeah, the Nameless Witch!" announced Aracely.

At that, Ter's eyes flew open, and the candle she was holding went out. She blinked as though seeing the room for the first time. Then she turned and started toward Riley and the others.

Her skin was still covered in that luminescent glow, and she moved as if in a dream, her steps slow and fluid, her head tilted slightly to one side. And though her eyes were still dark blue, the look in them was empty. She looked, Riley thought, like a ghost.

"What is she doing?" Dhonielle shrank behind Riley, voice quivering.

Before Riley could answer, Great Callahan was there, crossing the room to approach Ter.

"Be careful, CeCe," Mama N said, shifting so that she stood closer to Riley and her prime, ready to defend them if needed.

Riley watched nervously as Mama C stood before Ter.

"Ter?" Mama C said. "Ter, can you hear me?"

Ter blinked, and for a second Riley thought the glow around her was dimming. Maybe everything would be okay. Maybe the spell had worked, and Ter was waking up.

But then she spoke, and the voice that came from her mouth was not the voice of a single child but the voices of multiple women braided together.

"Great Callahan," said the voices, drawing the words out slowly. "Mom. CeCe. These are your names."

Mama C opened her mouth to respond, then froze. A look of surprise widened in her eyes, and she answered, "Yes."

"Give them to me," the braided voices said.

And before anyone could react, Mama C's magic glowed brightly in her chest, swirling and coalescing like a star, before it flew into Ter's waiting hands.

"Cecelia!" shouted Mama N.

Mama C blinked, turning slowly around to face her wife, as though moving against a great force.

The witch smiled and said, "Your will belongs to me."

IF YOU GIVE A WITCH YOUR NAME . . .

If you give a witch your name
You know just what she'll do
Once she knows the words to use
She will destroy you
She'll take your heart, your soul she'll own
Double dee, hubble dee, bubble dee, ditch
You'll give her everything, down to your bones
That's the way of the Nameless Witch

25

THE NAMELESS WOLVES

Riley stood rooted to the ground. She was aware that all around her, people were calling out commands or gasping in shock, but she couldn't tear her eyes away from the sight of her mother, the fight gone from her eyes.

"Get them out of here!" shouted Uncle Will.

"William." Though it was Ter's mouth that moved, it still wasn't her voice. "Stop."

Uncle Will stopped moving abruptly, as though he were physically incapable of doing otherwise. It was strange to see his muscled form stuck midmotion, one arm thrown out toward his daughter, the other clenched tight by his side.

"This is your name," said the many voices. "Give me your others."

"W-Will . . . Anderson . . . Dad." Uncle Will resisted so hard that each name came out as a gasp.

"Give them to me," Ter said.

And just as with Mama C, Uncle Will's magic drew together and spun out of his chest into Ter's waiting hands. It happened in the blink of an eye. Then his shoulders slumped. He blinked. And he waited.

"Sit," the Nameless Witch commanded.

"What do we do?" Lydia asked, reaching for Riley with one hand and pulling Dhonielle close with the other.

Mama C still hadn't moved. She stood exactly where she'd been, while Uncle Will headed toward the fireplace and took a seat in a chair. He stared into the flames, as though entranced.

"I—I don't know," Riley said.

Mama N pressed a finger to her lips. "No words," she said in a whisper so soft it was almost inaudible. "No names."

Aunt Alexis whistled to get their attention. Then, tearing a strip of cloth from the hem of her shirt, she gestured for Bethany Books to move to the other side of the room.

Mama N remained exactly where she was, arms spread wide as if to hide them from view, while Bethany Books and Aunt Alexis moved around to either side of Ter. Riley understood all at once that they were going to try and overwhelm her, then stop her from speaking.

Ter seemed to come to the same conclusion, because before they could move, she rushed forward. Straight at Aunt Alexis, who shifted instantly into a wolf and bared her teeth in warning.

Ter veered around Aunt Alexis, and then she did something truly unexpected.

She stepped up to the wall where the names of all their ancestors were carved in glowing lithodust, and then she pressed her hands against it.

"These are their names," she said, voices snaking around the room. "Give them to me."

Every name carved into the wall glowed brilliantly gold, then began to flow toward Ter, like water through a drain.

"Sweet moons, no!" cried Bethany Books. Then she shifted into her wolf and howled. It was an attack, and she aimed the sound directly at Ter.

It hit Ter squarely between the shoulder blades, knocking her forward. A call like that would have floored a full-grown wolf, but Ter shook it off as though it were little more than a vigorous slap on the back. The names continued draining toward her hands, faster now, in spite of Bethany's attack.

"Give them to me!" the many voices demanded.

The wall shone vibrantly, violently gold.

"Stop," the many voices hissed through the room.

Bethany Books made a strangled sound and collapsed to the floor, all four legs going limp. Mama N started toward her, then suddenly stopped, as though she'd forgotten what she was about to do. And across the room, Aunt Alexis whimpered and slid down onto her haunches.

Then, all at once, the wall went dark. The only light came from the blazing fire, the only sounds the snapping of its flames, the popping of its logs, and a slow, rasping breath from the middle of the room, where Ter now swayed back and forth.

No one dared to move.

What just happened? Aracely asked.

She took their names, Kenver answered in disbelief.

Whose names? Dhonielle asked.

All of them. Lydia's voice was hard. *The names of all our ancestors.*

In the flickering light, Riley spotted Mama N. She had crouched next to Bethany Books and was stroking her fur, but whether it was to soothe the wolf or calm the confusion in her own mind, Riley couldn't tell.

Feeling horrified and numb, she said, *She took them all.*

SO MUCH FOR LUCK

*B*ut *only the Nameless Witch can do that,* Aracely pro-tested. *Sweet moons, she's the Nameless Witch!*

How did that happen? Lydia asked. *And why didn't she take our names?*

She repeated the question, but Riley had no idea how to answer it. That, and it seemed a little less pressing than the other question on her mind: *How do we get out of here?*

There were no adults left here to help. The Nameless Witch had control of all of them. And they were each between the pack and the door.

Ter stood in the dead center of the room. There was no way to get past her without getting caught.

She hadn't moved in a few minutes, though, so Riley hoped that meant they had some time to figure it out.

Maybe we're just lucky? suggested Aracely.

It's never been the case before, muttered Dhonielle.

Except it kind of has been. Kenver shifted closer to the group. *Ever since the Devourer. Which, okay, wasn't lucky, but it does make us different. We're the Winter Pack. Maybe that means something.*

Aracely held up a finger. *We did have a vision of Ter before we found her. Maybe we weren't supposed to help her at all. Maybe we were supposed to defeat her, the same way we did the Devouring Wolf.*

Riley shifted on her feet. She couldn't ignore how much sense that made, but she also didn't like it. Ter wasn't like the Devourer. She hadn't chosen any part of this. She wasn't bad the way the Devourer had been bad. She was good. And in spite of everything, Riley still wanted to help her.

But they wouldn't be able to help anyone if they didn't find a way to escape.

We have to get out of here, she said, searching for anything that might help them do just that. *Why aren't there any windows in here?*

Aracely grinned. *We could make one.*

Why do you always go for destructive solutions? Dhonielle said.

Sometimes they're the best ones. Aracely shrugged. *I don't make the rules. Besides, exploding a wall is so much better than exploding a harmless, helpless teddy bear.*

I've always wanted to burst out of a building like the Kool-Aid Man, Kenver added, with a smile.

Okay. But if we're going to do this, we need to act fast. Lydia pointed a finger back toward Ter.

The young witch had turned and was now staring straight at them.

No, not at all of them. At Riley.

Something stirred in Riley's chest. And it wasn't fear, which surprised her. Some part of her brain acknowledged that fear was probably the most appropriate response. But Riley felt something else.

"Hang on," she said, rising from her crouched position and taking a step toward Ter.

Riley! her prime called together.

"It's okay," she said, even though she wasn't entirely sure about that. Just mostly. There was a feeling in her gut that told her this was the right thing to do. Ter knew her name—at least she had known it before they performed the rite—but she hadn't used it. Maybe that meant she was still in there, waiting for them to help her.

If that was the case, then Riley needed to be brave right now. She needed to take this risk. Not only for Ter, but for her moms, her aunt and uncle, and the rest of their pack.

"Ter?" Riley stepped cautiously toward the witch. Then again. And when the witch didn't move, she took another step and another, until she was only a few feet away.

Ter's gaze followed Riley's every move. Her eyes were both hard and hollow, but something about them felt familiar to Riley.

"Ter?" she said again, softer this time.

The girl blinked, and for a second, Riley thought she saw a flash of recognition in her eyes. Then she opened her mouth and spoke.

"Riley," said the many voices.

Riley's breath froze in her throat. Fear shot from the crown of her head to the tips of her toes. She tensed, expecting to lose both her name and her magic in the next second. Ter was gone. There was only the Nameless Witch. Riley had been wrong to trust her gut. And now her prime would suffer for her mistake.

But after a few seconds, Riley realized that nothing was happening. She was fine. Her magic was still where it should be and, as far as she could tell, so was her name.

"I'm Riley Callahan," she said, pressing her hands to her chest.

Suddenly, Ter gasped, drawing in a breath as though she'd been suffocating. Her hand shot out to Riley's, clasping it tight.

"Help me, Riley," Ter's voice—and *only* Ter's voice—said.

"I don't know how!" cried Riley. "Tell me how!"

But at that moment, the doors of the Hall of Ancestors flew open and a man burst inside. Then he raised a bow, armed with an arrow with a glowing green tip.

"So much for lucky," Aracely muttered.

Riley barely had time to acknowledge that a hunter had made it inside the wards, before he took aim and fired.

27

ESCAPE

Riley saw a streak of green flying straight for her. She felt Ter pulling her close, and then she saw the arrow explode in thin air. It took her a second to understand that the glow surrounding Ter wasn't just pretty. It was protection.

"Thanks," Riley said in a shaky voice.

Ter nodded, expression pinched with pain, like it was taking a lot of effort to hold on to herself.

In the doorway, the hunter had reloaded his bow and was aiming at them again. He was ignoring the adults, who were all still stuck in the magic of the Nameless Witch.

"Now!" shouted Riley.

She grabbed Ter's hand, and together they raced toward the rest of the prime pack. The others were already howling, targeting a spot in the wall as they searched for the frequency that would allow them to blast a hole.

Adding her voice to theirs, Riley tried to ignore

the arrow exploding in her peripheral vision. Ter was keeping them safe, but Riley had no idea how long that would last.

They had to hurry.

But they also had to do this right.

Just as a third arrow exploded in a flash of green, they found the right note. Their voices came together, resonating with the stones in the wall. They called louder and louder, until it was as if their voices had become a massive fist. It punched through the wall, leaving a hole just large enough for them to climb through.

"Go!" shouted Riley, giving Dhonielle a shove. She scrambled through quickly, then reached back to take Kenver's hand.

A fourth arrow exploded and, right on its heels, a fifth.

"Riley," Ter said. "Too many. I can't—"

Riley turned to see the hunter making his way toward them with powerful strides, another arrow notched against his bow.

Kenver was through the hole, and Aracely was next. But Riley had the horrible realization that even if they all made it through, the hunter would be right behind them. They would never escape.

Then a low growl echoed through the hall. The hunter paused, turning on his heel to search for the source. Riley found it first, and her heart swelled to see Milo and

Teddy, their heads tucked low, their teeth bared, their eyes locked on the hunter.

They'd been outside when the Nameless Witch was taking names, so now they were still able to fight.

"Go!" Riley said again. This time, she pushed Ter ahead of her.

She heard the low twang of the hunter's bow and the snapping growl of her brother, and then both she and Ter were through the hole and running toward the woods.

Riley was a little startled to see that it was still daylight. The clouds were thick, and it was snowing, but it was barely past noon. So much had happened in so little time this morning. It was hard to believe it was still the new moon.

"Where are we going?" Lydia asked.

Riley wished she had an answer to that question, but so far, all she knew was that they had to keep running.

"He's after *me*," Ter gasped out. "Leave me here and go."

"No," Riley answered automatically. "We're not leaving you behind. We just need a place to hide."

"I hate to add pressure, but we really need to be moving faster," Lydia said.

"Can you fly?" Riley asked Ter.

In answer, Ter rose from the ground and darted off, wending through the trees.

Riley dove forward, shifting in midstride. Her shoulders curled toward the ground, and by the time she landed, she caught herself on paws instead of hands.

On either side, Lydia and Aracely, Dhonielle and Kenver, shifted just as smoothly into wolves. And the five of them raced through the woods as the snow drifted down around them.

Riley's heart pounded with every step. Ter was a shimmering star above them, but even from this distance, Riley could tell she was struggling. The eight Nameless Witches who had come before her were all there with Ter. Inside her mind. And they were trying to fold her in with them. Somehow, the New Moon Rite had accelerated their spell, but it wasn't complete. Riley didn't know how to explain it, but whatever it was that had connected Ter to the five wolves in the Winter Pack before she'd ever crossed into Wax & Wayne, it was still there. Helping Ter resist the spell.

It gave Riley hope that they could reverse it. If they could just find someplace safe, where they could stop and think.

And, suddenly, she knew exactly where to go.

She yipped to get Ter's attention, and then she turned her steps for home.

28

DING-DONG!

Riley had never felt as safe anywhere as she did at home. But without her moms there, the Callahan house felt empty and cold, even with all the lights turned on and the heater rumbling in the background.

They'd piled through the front door in a heap and slammed it shut behind them. Then, when they'd been sure that no hunter was going to come crashing through on their heels, they'd moved into the kitchen, where Lydia got to work boiling milk for hot chocolate and Kenver found a stack of blank paper so they could write down everything they knew to be true. So far, the paper had three items on it:

    1. Ter was the Nameless Witch.

    2. Ter was also not *entirely* the Nameless Witch.

    3. A hunter was looking for her.

Riley thought that they knew a bit more than that, but Kenver had set the pen down several minutes ago and had been staring at those three items ever since, a look of intense fear on their face. Riley had decided that the list was long enough.

Besides, she knew how Kenver felt. She had just watched both of her moms, her aunt, her uncle, and Bethany Books all succumb to the power of the Nameless Witch, and she had no idea how to help them.

"What do we do? What do we do? What do we do?" Dhonielle had been muttering this under her breath for approximately five whole minutes.

The only response was the scrape of Lydia's spoon on the pot as she stirred cocoa powder into simmering milk.

Riley didn't have an answer. None of them did. All they had was this collective feeling of hopelessness. Who could help them now?

Just then, the front door banged open. Dhonielle shrieked, Lydia spilled some cocoa on the stove, and Riley shot to her feet, but it was only Milo, Teddy, and the rest of their prime. The five of them raced into the house, slamming the door behind them.

"Does anyone want to explain what just happened back there?" shouted Teddy.

"You didn't lead that hunter straight here, did you?" Aracely snapped, hurrying to peer through the living room windows.

"Of course not," Teddy snapped right back. "We chased him off of you and then gave him the runaround."

"We looped through the South Wood," Milo explained.

"And we figured you'd come back here. I mean, we hoped you would."

"And we were right, so can someone please explain things now and—whoa!" Teddy, who had been striding into the kitchen to help himself to a cup of hot cocoa, jumped back at the sight of Ter sitting at the table.

She'd been silent since they'd arrived, with her hands clenched tightly together and an expression of pain on her face. Every once in a while, she looked at Riley or Lydia or Dhonielle, and it seemed to help her. Just a little.

"You brought her with you?" Milo said. "But she just—she just—"

"This isn't her fault." Riley moved to Ter's side.

"Of course it is!" If Teddy had been a volcano, he would have spewed hot lava all over the table. "Would any of this have happened if she hadn't come here? No. Therefore, it's her fault," he said, answering his own question.

"You don't know what you're talking about," Riley said.

"You're right." Teddy crossed his arms over his chest. "What I know is that you five were keeping a secret from everyone because you think you're so special, and now you've ruined everything."

"Riley." A whisper came from behind her.

"That's not why we kept the secret!" protested Riley.

"Yes, it is," Milo said, stepping in. "You thought you knew better than everyone else, that you had a solution, because you defeated the Devourer. And just look at what's happened! Our parents, Dhonielle's parents, they're under her spell! Who knows if we'll ever get them back! All because you five think you're special!"

"Riley." The whisper came again.

"You know what? You're right." Riley's anger simmered, hot and steady. She'd spent so much time worried that everyone else thought they were special, that she'd never stopped to realize that maybe it was true. "We *are* special! That's why this is happening to us, and you can either help us figure it out, or get out of the way."

Milo blinked in surprise, but he no longer looked angry and that was an improvement.

"Riley." This time, Ter's voice was louder, fractured at the edges in a way that had become sickeningly familiar.

Ter's face was pinched, sweat dampened her temples, and she was breathing quickly.

"What is it, Ter?" Riley said, as calmly as she could.

Before Ter could answer, there was a shift in her expression. Her eyes darkened, just as they had in the Hall of Ancestors, and a faint glow surrounded her hands. Then a smile that was not Ter's smile spread across her lips, and her eyes locked onto Teddy.

"Hello, little wolf," said the many voices of the Nameless Witch.

Teddy stumbled back into the wall, his mouth gaping open like a fish's.

"Your name is—"

Aracely released a sudden, earsplitting scream, which blocked out anything the Nameless Witch might have said next.

"Out! Now!" bellowed Riley, shoving first Teddy, then Milo before her. "All of you! Your entire pack! Upstairs! Plug your ears!"

They didn't argue. Clapping their hands over their ears, they did exactly as Riley had said, and hurried up the stairs to Milo's room, where they would be unable to hear if anyone said their names.

As soon as Teddy and Milo's pack was gone, Ter wilted. Her eyes returned to their usual dark blue, and the glow faded from her hands. She looked exhausted.

"Are you okay?" Riley asked.

"I'm sorry," Ter whispered. Her hands were clasped so tightly together that her knuckles were blanched as white as snow.

"It's okay," Riley assured her. "They're safe. It's okay."

"It's not, though," Kenver said. "She learned all our names back there. She can control every single wolf in our pack if she has the chance. What are we supposed to do about that?"

"Except us," Dhonielle said.

"Huh?" Kenver asked.

"Except us. She can control any wolf in our pack except for us, for some reason." Dhonielle turned to look at Riley, then added, "Because we're special."

There was something exciting about using the word to describe themselves. It didn't feel like an insult or an attack, it felt like something that made them unique and maybe even a little powerful.

"I wish being special came with a handbook," Kenver muttered.

"That would make finding a solution to this mess a lot easier." Lydia brought six mugs of steaming hot chocolate to the table. "Think I should make some for them?" she asked, looking toward the second story.

"I'll do it," Dhonielle volunteered. She pushed back from the table and ducked into the kitchen.

Riley suspected she just wanted an excuse to think about something other than her parents, and she didn't blame her. Everywhere Riley looked, she was reminded of her moms. From the dirty coffee mugs still resting by the sink to the growing grocery list on the narrow whiteboard by the light switch. They needed more eggs, because they always needed eggs, and more Cholula, which was Mama N's favorite hot sauce in the whole world.

And sitting next to Riley was the person who had taken her moms away from her. Riley still believed that it wasn't Ter's fault, the same way it hadn't been Mama C's fault that the Devourer had stolen her face and then used it to terrorize the new wolves last summer. They were both the victim of magic spells they hadn't cast, and they had both needed help to get free of them. Helping Ter had been the right thing to do.

But it was hard not to feel a little helpless. And a little to blame.

"I don't know what to do," Riley admitted.

"You'll think of something," Aracely said, as warmly as she could manage, given the circumstances. "That's what you do."

"It's what we do," Riley corrected. She knew Aracely was right, they would think of something, she only wished she knew where to start.

Just then, the doorbell rang: *Ding-dong! Ding-dong!*

"The hunter!" whisper-shouted Dhonielle, a spoon brandished in one hand like a weapon.

"I doubt a hunter would ring the bell," Kenver said.

"Or maybe they would assume that's what we would think," Aracely added, "and then ring the bell to lure us out."

"I'll get it," said Lydia.

Riley followed her, not entirely sure that this was a good idea.

And the instant Lydia pulled open the door, she was convinced it was the exact opposite: a very bad idea.

There, standing on the porch, were two familiar and entirely unwelcome faces.

Robin Mercy and Justina Welsh.

At the sight of them, Robin raised a glass orb cupped between her palms.

"Make safe this space, with every bit of haste!" she called.

Before Riley could react, the orb shimmered, its edges blurring and expanding rapidly. It passed over Riley and the others, through the living room and the kitchen, right into the backyard, where it stopped. It shimmered again, and its edges hardened to glass once more, trapping the entire house inside a dome.

Justina fixed Riley with a hard gaze and said, "Inside, pups. We need to talk."

"Please don't panic. We've only come to help," Robin Mercy said, smiling gently at them.

"Help who?" demanded Riley.

"You," Robin said. Then her eyes flicked to a point over her shoulder. "And her."

"Hi, Aunt Robin," Ter said.

With a smile, Robin stepped forward and took Ter's hands. "Such precious eyes we use to weep, close them now and go to sleep."

As soon as Robin had finished speaking, Ter fainted. Aracely barely managed to catch her before she hit the floor.

29

POLITICS, MAGIC & DANGER

They moved Ter onto the couch.

"She's exhausted," Robin said, brushing Ter's hair away from her face. "She's working very hard right now, and she's going to need her energy for what comes next. The sleep will help with that."

"You're her aunt?" Riley narrowed her eyes at Robin, unsure what to think of this woman who had just rolled into the room and cast a spell on Ter.

"I am," Robin confirmed. "And I promise you I mean her no harm."

"Does this mean you're related to Darren Grimsley, too?" Dhonielle asked.

Robin pursed her lips and gave a tight nod. "He's too much like his mother, and living out there with the Flint Witches has given him an ugly edge. But don't think too poorly of him. Ever since he was a boy, he's had to prove that he has what it takes to be a real witch. The Flints still have a hard time believing that boys make good witches."

"Why?" Riley asked.

"Oh, because sometimes tradition feels more important than it is."

"And because people don't like to share their power," Justina added. "Especially when they feel entitled to it."

Riley thought about what it must have been like for Darren, growing up with people who doubted him, and she did feel a little sorry for him. It reminded her of how she'd felt when she didn't turn into a wolf when she was supposed to, of that taunting refrain in her head telling her she wasn't a real wolf. But she'd found her pack and learned that the transformation was only part of what made her a wolf, and that had helped. It would have been much, much harder without them.

"Is it safe to come down now?" Milo called from the stairway.

"Who's this?" Robin asked, with a bright smile.

"My brother," Riley answered. Then to Milo she said, "It's safe. She's asleep."

"Who are you?" demanded Teddy, clomping down the stairs after Milo. Behind them came the other three: Heidi, Shannon, and Xavier. They arrived with their hands raised, in anticipation of needing to plug their ears again.

"Witches," Justina answered. "Good ones. And we're running out of time."

"For what?" Milo asked.

"To fix what *they* started," Justina said, tipping her head toward Riley. "Before someone else does it for them."

"What do you mean?" Lydia said. "What do you mean we started something?"

"The New Moon Rite," Kenver said. "It worked, but only partway."

"It wasn't a bad approach," Justina conceded with a nod. "But it was more wolf than witch."

"Well, so are we," Kenver responded, with a frown.

"So you are." Robin's laugh was almost like a cackle. "What you did was start the process. And if she were a normal witch, it might have worked, but by starting the process, you opened a door to an excessive amount of power. The New Moon Rite couldn't compete with the spell that was already in place."

"But why did it make things worse?" Riley asked, still confused.

"Think of it like a dam on a lake, where the water is at different levels on either side of the dam," Justina said.

Kenver bobbed their head, already into the exercise.

"You were looking at Ter and seeing one side of the dam, the side with less water, less power. But in order for your spell to work, you had to move the dam. And when you did . . ."

"The water from the other side rushed in," Kenver finished, always quick to understand magic and metaphors. "Wait. Does that mean we . . . Did we kill the other Nameless Witch?"

Robin made a face and puffed out a breath. "Her death was tied to the transfer of power. The spell is what ended her life. It just happened a bit sooner than we expected."

Riley stomach pitched. "You're saying that the Nameless Witch was the dam?"

Justina nodded. "And all of her power was on the other side," she said.

"But she's still Ter. She still knows who she is," Dhonielle said. "So did we stop it halfway or something?"

Robin tipped her head side to side. "Sort of. What you've done is to drive a wedge between Ter and the Nameless Witches who came before. It's why Ter is still able to be with us. Because she's holding on to you. But she's working very hard to stay here with us."

"Pretty soon, she won't be able to," Justina said, "and the spell will complete itself." She glanced sadly at Ter, still lying on the couch with her eyes closed.

"And Ter?" Riley asked.

"And Ter," Robin said, "will become nameless. A danger to wolves and witches alike. And we'll be forced to deliver her to the tower if we can't complete the severing."

"You would lock her up?" Riley asked in horror.

"For our safety and yours," Justina said swiftly. "If she has learned any names while she's been here, then the danger to your pack is very real."

"She knows our names," Milo said from his spot on the stairs. He and the others had been so quiet Riley had nearly forgotten they were there. But the five of them were clustered together, listening to every terrible word.

"What did you say?" Robin asked.

"She knows our names already." Milo pointed at Ter's sleeping form.

"Whose names?" Justina's tone had become deadly serious.

"All of them," Lydia said. "She took them from the Hall of Ancestors. All at once. She just . . . drained them from the walls."

Robin and Justina shared a silent look.

"Then there is no more time to waste," Robin said.

"But if you want us to sever the spell, then why did you bring the Flint Witches here?" Dhonielle said, sounding suspicious. "We thought you were working with them."

"Not exactly," said Robin, turning to Justina.

"Witch politics are complicated. I'm sure wolf politics are just as complicated, but we—the Free Witches—haven't always been in lockstep with the more traditional covens," Justina explained. "There was a time and a place for the Nameless Witch, but these days, people aren't going around burning witches at the stake. We have other things to worry about, and we believe that no one—not a single person or a coven—should be able to choose when someone comes into their power. We'd much rather have a solution that puts a pin in when it's supposed to happen so that witches can control where they'll be. The way wolves do."

"That and the spell has only become more dangerous over the years," Robin added. "The spell has an echo that resonates through time, one that only the current Nameless Witch can hear."

"Kind of like the last call of First Wolf," Riley said, putting the pieces together.

"Yes, almost exactly like that, but focused on a single person. Our theory is that over time, the message of that echo has lost some of its original purpose, which was to become a funnel for witch magic," Robin explained.

"Now it's more destructive," Justina said, taking over naturally, the way Riley's moms sometimes did when they were telling a story. "The message is something like: Control all magic. And that's what the Nameless Witch has started to do unless she's captured and imprisoned for her lifetime. We don't see this as a sustainable solution, but there are plenty of people who do."

Robin looked toward her niece with a heavy expression. "No one should have to endure such a terrible thing."

"Which is why we came to find Ter when we did. We just didn't count on a group of young wolves getting there first," Justina finished.

"So what happens now?" Riley asked.

"Now, you have a decision to make." Robin said it like it was an apology, even though she hadn't apologized for anything. "Either you attempt to complete the severing and prevent Ter from becoming the Nameless Witch, or you do nothing and we take her to the tower, where the spell will complete itself and Ter will live out the rest of her days."

"How is that even a choice? Of course we'll complete the spell," Riley said.

"Before you decide, there are a few more things you need to know."

"It's dangerous, isn't it?" Dhonielle asked.

"And it has to be us?" Kenver added. "Because we started the spell?"

"It is, and it does." Robin wasn't smiling anymore.

"What kind of dangerous?" Aracely asked.

"There is both political and magical danger." Robin held up a finger. "Political because we do not represent all witches but what we are asking you to do will affect them, and there will be those who don't agree with us and who will likely blame wolves for interfering."

Lydia cautiously raised a hand. "We're not leaders.

We're not even adults. We can't make those kinds of decisions. Can we?"

Riley swallowed hard. There were no adults here to ask and no time to find others. "What about the *magical* dangers?" she asked.

"Those are a little harder to pin down, because the truth is, we don't know." Justina leaned her back against the front door, arms crossed over her chest. "There could be a whole lot of nothing, or there could be all kinds of magical shock waves. And there's more." Justina pushed away from the door and paced into the middle of the room. "We also don't know what will happen to you. Again, maybe nothing, but there's also another possibility."

"What kind of possibility?" Dhonielle was doing her best not to look afraid, but Riley could see the tension in her shoulders.

"Well, since the six of you are already locked together, and since the point of the spell is to release Ter's magic, it could also mean releasing yours."

Silence filled the room, and Riley felt a pressure building in her chest.

"We could . . . lose our magic?" Aracely said.

"It's possible." Justina's mouth flashed in and out of a frown. "We just don't know. And we want to make sure you go into this decision with your eyes wide open."

"So you're saying all of this is up to the five of us?

That we have to choose whether or not Ter becomes the Nameless Witch, even if it means losing our own magic?" Riley asked. Even though she was pretty sure that's what they meant, she needed to hear it again. "We have to choose?"

"That's exactly what we're saying," Robin said, sympathy in every syllable.

"What's more," Justina added, "we need you to decide now."

30

AN IMPOSSIBLE CHOICE

The witches stepped outside, giving them a few moments to make what was perhaps the single most devastating decision Riley could imagine.

"So on the one hand"—Kenver held a hand in the air, palm up—"we do the spell, stop Ter from becoming the Nameless Witch, and risk . . . literally everything, including our own magic and all of wolf-witch relations for years to come. And on the other . . ." Kenver held out their other hand.

"The Nameless Witch rises again," Aracely said, "and takes control of our parents and uses our pack for magic parts." She looked around the room at everyone. "Right?"

Everyone held their breath until Kenver started up again.

"I was going to say: on the other hand, Ter becomes the Nameless Witch and we never see her again. Just like we've never seen any other Nameless Witch."

Teddy raised his hand to speak. "But what about our

names?" he said, and for the first time in recent memory, he wasn't looking at them like he was angry or jealous. "Can we really trust witches to do what they say? If they don't lock her up, then she'll come for us, right?"

"She already has control of our moms." Milo's voice was tight, like he was trying not to cry. "She could make them do anything she wants."

On the couch, Ter shifted and made a small whimpering sound. Milo and Teddy jumped in response, and all five of their prime slapped their hands over their ears.

"It's okay," Lydia said. "She's still asleep."

"She's still fighting," Riley added. Because that's exactly what Ter was doing. She was fighting to hold on to herself, to keep everyone around her safe. "We should, too."

"But . . . I don't want to lose my magic," Kenver said, their hands curled into tight fists. They shrugged. "I'm sorry, but I don't."

"They didn't say that would happen for sure," said Lydia.

"They said it *could*," Kenver bit back. "And magic is one of the only things that makes me feel like me."

"Well, if we don't do this, then something even worse could happen to more people," Aracely said.

Dhonielle groaned. "This isn't a choice at all. It's a terrible situation that we're only in because we tried to help someone. It's not fair."

Riley agreed. It wasn't fair. It wasn't the way things were supposed to work. When you did a good thing, good things were supposed to happen to you. But they'd done a good thing, and all that had happened were bad things. Negative consequences and impossible choices.

Mama C always said that choice was wolves' most sacred magic, but right now it felt more like a burden. Riley didn't want to have to make this big choice. She was too young, too inexperienced, too unimportant.

Then she looked at Ter, and her heart squeezed once more.

Riley knew what it was like to have no choice. No one had asked her and the others if they wanted to become the Winter Pack. It had simply happened to them. Just like it was happening to Ter. Just like all the Nameless Witches before her, she'd been told that this was her duty, that all of her choices were going to be taken away, in service of a spell that was cast hundreds of years ago.

Her options had been just as terrible as theirs were now: become the Nameless Witch and lose herself, or run and lose everything else.

Helping Ter hadn't been Riley's responsibility, but she didn't regret it. Not even now.

"It may not seem like a choice, but it is," Riley said, turning to face the group. "This is our chance to make sure every wolf *and* every witch has the ability to make choices for themselves."

Since becoming a wolf, Riley had felt more grown-up than ever before. Not only that, but the transformation had changed the way other people looked at her. How they looked at her whole prime. The adults looked at them like they were waiting for them to vanish or sprout horns or something. But their peers looked at them like they were different, had used those differences against them, like being special was a bad thing. Right now, though, it felt important. They were the only ones who could make this choice, the only ones who could take this risk to save their entire pack. And she believed they could do it. She believed in her prime pack and all the wolves of the Hackberry Hill Alliance. She believed in her moms and her two siblings. She believed in Ter. And she believed that everyone deserved to choose who they wanted to be.

She and the others hadn't chosen to become the Winter Pack, but they could choose how to use the power it gave them.

"Even if the worst happens and our magic is severed with hers, we'll still have each other. We'll still have our pack."

Riley turned and caught the eyes of each of her prime, one by one. In them, she saw her own decision reflected.

"Okay," Lydia said. "I'm in."

"Me too," said Aracely, twisting her long, dark curls up into a ponytail that meant business.

"Yeah, I'm in," Dhonielle confirmed.

They all turned to Kenver. Kenver's lips were pinched, and they looked like they'd swallowed something sour, but they nodded. "Okay."

Movement from the stairwell caught Riley's eye and she turned to find Teddy with his hand in the air like he was in class. Milo sat just over his shoulder, looking pale and scared.

"Um, yes?" Riley said.

"For what it's worth, I'm sorry for making fun of you." Teddy cleared his throat. "Can we help?"

Riley smiled. "We've got this." Then she pulled open the front door and announced, "We'll do it. If you can show us how, we'll complete the severing."

INTERRUPTED

For the third time today, Riley, Lydia, Dhonielle, Kenver, and Aracely were prepared to unwitch Ter. This time, though, they knew what they were doing. Or at least they had people with them who knew what they were doing, and that was basically the same thing.

"The Severing Spell requires that you each give Ter your names," Robin Mercy was explaining. "This will complete the bond that is already forming between the six of you and sever her connection to the original Nameless Witch Spell."

"Sorry, I don't mean to be difficult, but doesn't she already know our names?" Lydia said. "Didn't she take them from the Hall of Ancestors?"

"Yep, she did." Justina was sitting in the middle of the room with Ter, who was still sleeping. "But there is a difference between learning your names from the world and receiving them from you. The name you *give* her ultimately has more power than one she reads on a wall or a piece of paper or overhears from a friend. Those are just starting points, and they do have power, but not enough for something like this."

That made sense to Riley, but there was still one thing that bothered her. "What makes you think she won't use our names against us once she has them?"

Robin and Justina met eyes for a moment. Then Robin turned a kind smile on Riley and said, "We're going to have to trust her on that. As you said, she hasn't done it yet."

It wasn't much, but it did mean something to Riley. Ter had known her name for days and hadn't used it once. Even now that she was fighting the urges of every Nameless Witch who'd come before her, she hadn't used it still.

"After that, Ter will have to offer you her name in return," Robin continued. "But the name she has is tied to the Nameless Witches. To complete the spell, she will need to give herself a new name."

"That's when things could get a little dicey," Justina added. "She will be at her most vulnerable then and her most dangerous. She's going to need each of you to hang on, to help her choose a new name."

"We understand if you don't want to try," Robin said in a quiet voice.

"I want to try," Riley said immediately. "Nothing will

ever change between wolves and witches if we don't start trusting each other. And I trust Ter."

"And we trust her," Lydia said, looking at the rest of her prime, who nodded in confirmation. She leaned a shoulder into Riley, and Riley felt that familiar flush in her cheeks.

"We trust them, too," Teddy called from the staircase. "And we want to help, if there's anything we can do," he said.

The change in Teddy was so sudden that part of Riley wondered if he was under some sort of witch's spell.

"Right now, the best thing for you to do is watch for any sign of trouble. As for you five," Justina said, getting the still-unconscious Ter to her feet, "I need you in a circle here. Hold hands."

"Right here in the living room?" Riley asked. "But I spilled a bowl of Cheerios over there last week!" It seemed wrong that something so important should happen between an overstuffed sofa and a TV.

"Right here," Justina confirmed. "Unless you have a stone circle in your backyard."

"We actually do," she said. "But I don't think Mama N will appreciate us tromping through her flower garden. Even if it is March."

Justina barked a laugh. "You know, not what I meant, but not too far off either. We'll stick with what we've got. It'll be warmer."

"Besides," Robin added, "sometimes mundane spaces make the best magic."

"I think I see something," Milo called from the living room window.

Robin was opening her mouth to reply when—

BOOM!

The house shook. Or, more accurately, the glass dome surrounding the house shook.

BOOM!

"Oh dear," Robin muttered, joining Milo to peer through the window. "I'm afraid we have company."

Justina didn't even have to look. She wore an expression of deep irritation when she said, "Freaking Flint Witches."

DAY INTO NIGHT

"**I**'m afraid you're going to have to do this on your own," Robin said. "We'll distract them for as long as we can. Give you as much time as possible."

"We'll help," Teddy announced, gesturing to his prime. Behind him, Milo gave a decisive nod, and Riley felt the distance between them grow just a little bit smaller.

Still, she told Teddy, "You should stay inside, where it's safe."

Teddy laughed. "And let the Winter Pack take all the credit? No way. You may be superannoying, but we've got your back." Riley was surprised to hear that when he called them the Winter Pack this time, there was no malice in his voice.

"Thank you," Riley said, one alpha to another.

BOOM! went the house.

Teddy gave a crooked smile as he shrugged. "You're the one we should be thanking."

Riley wished there were time to answer him, but she

was also kind of glad there wasn't. She didn't really know what to do with warm feelings about Teddy Griffin.

"We need to do this now. You know what to do," Justina said, and it wasn't a question.

"We give her our names," Riley answered. "All of them. And then we help her choose a new one for herself."

"Right. Here we go." Robin blinked back tears and took Ter by the shoulders. "The rain is falling, the trees do shake, the storm is coming and it's time to wake!"

Ter's eyes fluttered, then snapped open wide. They were dark and unfocused—and wrong.

"Ter?" Riley said, but she could already see it wasn't her. Instinctively, she took a step back. "What's happening to her?"

"I—I don't—" Robin didn't finish her sentence, because at that moment, Ter's hands began to glow.

White and purple and green smoke swirled around and through her fingers. Her eyes turned a deep, inky purple, with a cold light in the center. She grinned and opened her hands, revealing a charm of bone wrapped in silver, attached to a leather cord.

Riley gasped. Her mother's talisman. The one the witches had returned to her and that had been around her neck ever since. She tried to remember if she'd seen it before they'd fled the Hall of Ancestors, but she wasn't sure. Had Ter snatched it and held on to it without meaning to?

An image of Ter seated at the kitchen table with her hands clutched before her flashed through Riley's mind.

Without warning, Ter pressed the talisman against Robin's chest. "Sleep," she hissed.

Robin's eyes closed instantly. Her chin tipped forward, and she fell to the ground and didn't move.

"Good bones." Ter's voice was once again the voice of many, frayed as though pressed through a sieve. The talisman was the only thing that did not glow. It was a flat eggshell white against her palm. "Strong bones."

"Pups!" Justina's voice was thin and sharp. But whatever she was going to say next was drowned out by a high-pitched shriek, coming from Ter.

She bolted toward the front door. Her voice was a hissing whisper, words tumbling over each other like waves, becoming indecipherable. The door exploded outward, sending wood chips flying in every direction, and then Ter was gone.

Riley followed. She could sense the rest of her prime coming with her, through the hole where a door once stood and onto the front porch. She skidded to a halt.

The front yard was filled with witches. At least a dozen, peppered all around. She spotted Darren, but she didn't recognize any of the others and she didn't have time to consider them.

Standing at the bottom of the porch steps was Ter. Riley couldn't see her expression, but whatever she was doing, she had the full attention of the witches.

"What do we do?" Milo asked, bumping into her from behind.

"Get back inside!" hissed Justina. But no one listened to her.

Ter raised a hand. The cord of the talisman was now wrapped around her fingers, the bone dangling exactly in the center of her palm. She whispered a single word, and there was a flash of purple light as Robin's protective dome dissolved around them.

"Darren Grimsley," the voices said. "You like power so much. Which one of your fingers has the greatest potential? Decide and then give it to me."

"Get inside," Justina hissed again, and even though her voice was pitched low, Ter turned toward her.

"Justina Welsh, Justina Welsh. You don't want me to exist anymore? What should I do with you?"

Behind Ter, three other witches were coming together. One of them held a metal sphere in her hands. She stretched it out before her, and all three of them locked their eyes on Ter, their lips moving swiftly as they cast a quiet spell.

The metal sphere began to grow in the same way Robin's protective sphere had done not so long ago. Then, just as they cast it toward Ter, she spun. She leapt into the air and came back down on top of the sphere, crushing it flat.

"Come on!" Riley raced down the steps and held her hands at her sides. Dhonielle grasped one, Kenver the other, with Aracely and Lydia completing the circle around Ter.

"Teralyn Grimsley, we know you're in there, and we want you to come back." Riley's voice shook, even though she was shouting. "Here are our—"

"You think you know how to win this fight, but I can turn day into night!" Ter clapped her hands over her head, and the entire world went dark.

THE SEVERING

Riley was flung back. She hit the ground hard, one elbow taking the full force of the impact. She blinked, then blinked again, but no matter how she rubbed her eyes, she couldn't see anything.

"Hello?" cried Dhonielle. She sounded very far away. Much farther than she had before the sun had gone out. "Riley?"

"I'm here!" answered Riley. "Where's everyone else?"

"Here!" called Lydia.

"Over here!" shouted Kenver.

"I'm somewhere!" added Aracely.

The Nameless Witch laughed. In the dark, it was a loud, echoing sound, which seemed to come from nowhere and everywhere all at once.

"Riley!" shouted Milo.

The Nameless Witch stopped laughing. "Milo Cecil Callahan," she said. "I knew your great-uncle. He was such a good pup. Did whatever I told him to. Just like you will."

"Yes," Milo said. His voice was calm now. Obedient.

"Milo! Cover your ears!" shouted Justina.

There was a brief flash of light as the witches attempted to push back the darkness.

The Nameless Witch laughed again, her voice skittering and scratching through the air like autumn leaves.

Riley wanted to scream. She wanted to dive at the Nameless Witch and make her stop talking. But she was trapped. Immobilized by the darkness around her.

She couldn't see anything. She couldn't find her prime. And without her prime, they couldn't complete the severing. She was lost in the dark, and so were they.

Except. Maybe that wasn't true.

Riley drew in a deep, calming breath and focused. This was just like the exercise she'd done with the bandanas in the woods, only this time, she didn't have as much time.

Stay where you are, she instructed. *I'm coming to you.*

She reached for Dhonielle's quick vibration first and followed it along as though it were a string. She tripped on a rock and got tangled in a bush, but eventually her hand landed on a familiar puffy coat.

You got me, Dhonielle said, gripping Riley's hand.

Riley breathed a quick sigh of relief and turned toward Kenver's calm resonance. This time, she moved more confidently, more sure of herself and her ability to find her prime.

Someone screamed in the dark, and there was another rush of movement and sound. Riley tuned it all out and headed for Aracely, then Lydia.

"Now what?" whispered Lydia.

"Now we complete the severing." Riley squeezed the hands that held hers, not sure who they belonged to.

"How?" squeaked Aracely. "We don't even know where Ter is."

"It doesn't matter where she is. She only needs to hear us," Riley answered, not sure how she knew this. "But this time, we stay together. Hold on tight, okay?"

Everyone agreed, clustering into a tight knot.

"I'll start," said Kenver. They drew in a deep breath and then raised their voice. "My name is Kenver Derry, and it is my truest name, though I have had several. My parents call me Any, which is kind of an inside joke, but they also call me Spark, because I love magic so much. These are my names. I give them to you in friendship and trust."

At first, there was no answer. Then, in the faintest whisper, they heard the fractured voices respond, "Kenver Derry."

"You next, Dhonielle," Riley urged.

Dhonielle cleared her throat. "Mine is Dhonielle Alexis Anderson. If you call me Danielle, I won't answer. This is my only name, and I give it to you in friendship and trust."

"Dhonielle Alexis Anderson," the voices answered. This time, Riley thought she could detect Ter's voice gaining strength, as though surfacing from a great depth.

Riley clenched her jaw at the sound.

"Lydia Marie Edgerton," Lydia said next, her voice clear as a bell. "I'm sorry I didn't give my name to you sooner, but I'm giving it to you now in friendship and trust."

Ter repeated the name. Her voice was stronger this time, but still struggling to hold on.

"You can do this, Ter," Riley said.

Behind her, Aracely took her turn. "Hi. My full name is Aracely Zoraida Bravo, though you probably already knew that. My sisters also call me Arazee, Celly, and Bingo. And sometimes I go by Arabella when it's easier, though that's usually just at Starbucks or something. Oh, and sometimes I'm Fossy. Not because of dancing or anything but because I love dinosaurs, and my tío thought it was funny to call me Little Fossil for a while, but then he shortened it." Aracely took a deep breath and paused as if to think of any other names she had. "These are all my names. I give them to you in friendship and trust."

"Aracely Zoraida Bravo," Ter repeated. Were there only two voices this time? Riley couldn't tell but it was her turn.

"I give you my names in friendship and trust," Riley called. She was surprised to hear the tremor in her own voice. "Riley Renée Callahan. Lilee to my siblings, and sometimes Ri to my friends. I told you to call me Winter because I wasn't supposed to give you a real name, but it is, because my pack is the Winter Pack. We're *your* pack, too, even though you aren't a wolf. But you're a part of it because *we* get to choose. Choice is a part of our magic, and it should be a part of yours, too!"

"Riley Callahan. Winter." Ter's voice was stronger than ever, the other voices fading beneath hers.

"What's your name?" called Riley, but this time, there was no answer. "What's your name?" she tried again, but again no answer came.

This was the moment Robin and Justina had warned them about. Now that they had severed Ter from the spell of the Nameless Witch, her name was gone and she was vulnerable. And dangerous.

"Tell us your name," said Riley.

"You get to choose," added Dhonielle.

Silence followed. Then, softly, they heard a voice in the darkness.

"My name," the voice said. "The name I choose is Spring."

The darkness around them began to fade. The sky eased from black to purple to wintery pale blue.

"Hello, Spring," said Riley, and she heard the greeting echoed by the other four in the circle.

There was no explosion. There was no dramatic flash

of light. Instead, eight whispering voices repeated, "Spring, Spring, Spring." The name swirled around them in the air, and then it changed, becoming other names.

"Irene Miller."

"Margaret Jones."

"Beverly McIntosh."

"Sarah. Rebekah. Elizabeth."

"Felicity Wallington."

"Honor Finch."

With a start, Riley realized what they were. These were the names of every Nameless Witch, all the way back to Honor Finch. The same witch who had cast the spell with First Wolf.

A gust of wind carried the names up and up and up, streams of rainbow-colored light traveling high, until they vanished in the sky.

Standing a few feet away was Spring. Head tipped up, watching, with a small smile on her face.

Then the lights faded, and it was as if everything inside of Riley faded, too. The last thing she saw was the rest of her prime and Spring slumping to the ground together.

IF YOU GIVE A WITCH YOUR NAME . . .

If you give a witch your name
There's one thing you should know
Once she knows the words to use
She'll never let you go
She'll take your hand and hold on tight
Double dee, hubble dee, bubble dee, bly
She'll seek you in the dark of night
And she'll teach you how to fly

BIG TROUBLE FOR LITTLE WOLVES

One day later, Riley was standing in the amphi-theater of Wax & Wayne surrounded by witches. A dozen of them. And at least half of them looked angry.

The other half were Free Witches, and they weren't angry. At least not with the wolves.

"This is an unprecedented and egregious breach of trust between witches and wolves," said a witch who had been introduced as Clementine Cryer and who'd walked into Wax & Wayne with such a look of disgust on her sharp features Riley wondered if she'd never been outdoors before. Even now, she stood as stiff as a board, like being so near to wolves was physically painful to her.

"There has never been trust between wolves and witches," Aunt Alexis snapped. In addition to Riley's prime pack, Aunt Alexis, Great Mort, and Great Callahan were the only wolves present. They'd wanted to keep this meeting small.

"Which is understandable when wolves behave like animals," Darren Grimsley said. He stood at Clementine Cryer's elbow, his face carved into that dangerous little smile.

Riley was really starting to hate that smile. She wished she could tell him so, but Great Callahan had told her, in no uncertain terms, that while she needed to be here, she was not to speak unless prompted.

It had been only a day since they'd stopped Spring from becoming the Nameless Witch and saved the entire wolf pack from living out the rest of their lives beholden to her whims. Somehow, it felt like it had been so much longer.

"We are here to find a solution we can all agree to, not trade uninspired barbs." Great Callahan didn't even look at Darren's smug expression. She stood tall before the witches, her voice level and so in control Riley could barely contain her urge to whoop aloud.

Instead, she schooled her own expression into one she hoped looked like her mom's, and met the stares of the witches who had come to complain about the Winter Pack.

"The solution is for the young wolves who created this mess to *uncreate* it," Clementine Cryer said. "I assume they know how to do that, since they were entrusted with a decision of such monumental importance."

This was the same argument she had been spouting for the last hour. She'd come in a huff, demanding to know who had cast the spell that had unraveled the magic of the Nameless Witch. When she'd realized that it hadn't been the work of a very powerful wolf, but the work of five wolves who were barely thirteen, she'd demanded that they clean up the mess they'd made. As if it were as simple as cleaning up their rooms.

"Clementine, we've been over this." Robin Mercy had stepped in, her voice soft and placating. "We must take into account—"

"I know what you think, Mercy," Clementine said sharply. "And I'm uninterested. The Free Witches have no say here and will be dealt with separately. My concern is with the immediate correction of this spell. And if the wolves who cast it are incapable of doing that, then we must have the girl. Your poor sister is so upset by all that's happened, she couldn't even leave her house."

Riley shifted on her feet and felt Dhonielle, at her side, do the same.

"Her name is Spring," Robin said, and even though her voice was gentle, it was firm. "And her wishes must be respected."

"She doesn't know what her wishes are. Her mind has been warped by these wolves." Clementine directed a brutal glance at Riley and the other wolves. "They've tricked her into thinking she's something she isn't."

Riley couldn't hold her words in any longer. "You're the ones who tricked her," she said, stepping forward with a sense of purpose. "She knows who she is and who she wants to be. All we did was make sure she could make those choices for herself."

Riley caught her mother's eye, ready to apologize for speaking out of turn. But instead of irritation in her mother's face, she saw approval. She saw love.

Great Callahan turned back to face Clementine Cryer. "My daughter is right. Spring asked us for help, and we gave it. As a pack. I understand that the results are not what you prefer, but until Spring wakes up and tells us what she wants, this is all just talk."

"She belongs at home." Clementine's voice was deeper and more menacing this time.

"I'm sure my poor sister would agree that Spring shouldn't be moved in her current condition." Robin said this as though any rational person would agree. "Especially if she, herself is struggling right now. I wouldn't want to burden her, or the Flint Witch coven, with the task of caring for someone who has just endured such a heroic trial."

"Heroic?" Darren spat the word.

"That's right," Robin answered. "Of course, I suppose that's not how everyone will see it."

There was something beneath Robin's words that Riley wasn't sure she understood, but suddenly,

Clementine didn't look so eager to take Spring away.

"Fine," said Clementine. "She can be your problem. At least until she wakes up."

"She's a child, not a problem." Though Great Callahan didn't move, the witches took a collective step back. Clementine Cryer looked ready to spit spells out of her eyes, and Darren Grimsley had finally stopped smirking. The Free Witches, on the other hand, looked pleased.

Justina Welsh clapped her hands once, drawing attention. "Welp! That seems to cover it. Spring is staying with her aunt Robin for the time being, since her mother hasn't made the trip. And since this pack is in Free Witch territory, that puts them under our protection, and we say they're good. Everything else is between us witches. So, Great Callahan, it's been a pleasure. We'll get out of your hair now." She paused suddenly. "That wasn't a joke or anything. Just an expression."

Great Callahan only nodded as the witches slowly took to the air. It was still strange to Riley to see them fly. They never rose too high—just high enough that they could skim through the trees without being noticed. It was breathtaking and ghostly all at once.

When they were gone, Great Callahan led the Winter Pack back to Clawroot. On the way, she walked with Riley, letting the four others go ahead.

"Do you think the Free Witches will really be able to protect Spring?" Riley asked.

"For the time being," Mama C answered.

"I wish she could stay with us." Riley had asked for Spring to stay with them approximately thirty-three times, but each time she'd been assured that Robin Mercy would take good care of her.

"She's still a witch, and she will have to find a way forward with her community. One way or another. And a lot of people aren't going to be happy with her. They have a lot to figure out."

"But it's better now. Or it will be soon." Now that the original spell had been broken, the Free Witches had a plan to replace it with one that was a lot like the spell First Wolf had created for wolves. Only instead of being tied to the night of the first full moon of summer, the witches would be tied to the last new moon of winter. "I don't understand why they don't all think it will be better. No one will have to give up who they are to keep their magic safe."

"I don't disagree with you," Mama C said. After a long silence, she added, "I'm proud of you, Riley."

Riley didn't know what to say to that, so she swallowed hard and didn't say anything at all.

"I assumed that you were being reckless. That you were making decisions without thinking them through. But I think I was wrong about that, so I owe you an apology: I'm sorry."

Riley really didn't know what to say to that. In fact, she was pretty sure her voice had turned into a little frog that was stuck in her throat. And she had no idea what was happening right now, so she kept quiet and kept walking.

"Trust is hard. And it's not permanent or stationary. It's like a puff of dandelion seeds. Sometimes it disperses on the wind, and when that happens, it can feel like it's hard to find. I think that's what's been happening to us. To you and me." She turned to take Riley's hands in her own. "I trust you, but I've also been treating you like a child. So in the future, I'm going to do better. I want you to trust that you can come to me with complicated issues and I'll consider them fairly. Okay?"

"Oh," said Riley. She was a little relieved to discover that her voice was still there and that it didn't sound like a frog at all. But more than that, she felt an overwhelming sense of pride. Her mom was saying that Riley's reasons for keeping Spring a secret had been complicated. Not right or wrong, but complicated. And she was saying that complicated was okay. Things weren't always completely right or completely wrong, completely one thing or another.

And that was okay.

"Yeah," Riley said. "Okay."

THE SPRING EQUINOX

It was two days before Spring woke up and Robin allowed her to get out of bed for a few minutes. It was another two days before she allowed her to leave the house, and only in the company of Riley and her prime.

Five wolves roved around the young witch's heels as they hurried from the outskirts of town onto the grounds of Wax & Wayne. Though it was still cold enough to turn their breath into puffs of white, the trees were rioting with tiny pink buds and the air smelled sweet and earthy with the promise of rain. They had a single purpose today and not much time before Robin would come looking for her niece.

She had been reluctant to let Spring out of her sight at all, but the instant she'd agreed, they'd made a run for it. Never giving her the chance to add caveats or conditions.

Finally, they were far enough that they stopped

running and all five wolves transformed back into their human forms.

"What do you need us to do?" Riley said.

"I think just be here?" Spring asked, though it wasn't really a question. "I don't know what will happen. Maybe nothing."

"But maybe something?" Aracely said.

Spring smiled fondly. "Maybe something. Hopefully, something."

"We're ready," Dhonielle said as the five of them fanned out in a circle around the witch. It was beginning to feel very familiar.

"We've got you," Kenver said.

"No matter what," Lydia added.

With a nod, Spring closed her eyes, focused, and took a deep breath. It had taken her several days to ask whether or not she could still do magic. No one had an answer for her. The only way to know for sure was to try.

At first, she hadn't wanted to try. She'd looked at Riley with watery dark blue eyes and asked, "But who would I be without my magic?"

And in a moment of clarity, Riley had answered, "You don't have to know."

Because the truth was, Riley didn't know that about herself either. She'd been a lot of things already—a child, a wolf, an alpha—and she still wasn't sure who she was. But she knew that the magic—which helped her turn from one thing to another, which connected her to people and places—was only part of the puzzle that made up Riley Callahan.

The truth was, she got to decide who she was every single day.

And so did Spring.

A cold wind swept through the field, tossing seeds from the tips of bearded winter wheat. Overhead, the clouds were thick and swirling gray, thrumming with a fresh storm. But today was the spring equinox. The day when the earth tipped from winter to spring, with equal amounts of daylight and darkness. It was a period of balance that could not last, because just like everything else, the earth wasn't only one thing, but many.

It was the perfect day for magic.

Riley squeezed her hands into small fists and watched as Spring concentrated. She knew what it felt like to want something and not get it. And she knew what it felt like to want something and get it. She desperately wanted that for Spring.

But as the seconds ticked by and nothing happened, Riley's hopes began to fall.

Maybe the Severing Spell had taken everything from Spring after all.

In spite of the cold, a thin line of sweat appeared on

Spring's lip. Still, try as she might, nothing happened. She could not work her magic.

Then, just as Riley was about to tell her to stop, Spring's eyes flew open. She gasped, and very slowly, she floated up until her toes were several inches from the ground.

She could still fly.

ACKNOWLEDGMENTS

Every new book is a journey and a dream and none of it is ever possible without the support of an agent like Lara Perkins. Thank you for always being there to hear the last call of First Wolf with me!

There are so many people at Razorbill who have worked to bring this werewolf community to readers. Thank you to everyone who has edited, copyedited, designed, and promoted this book. And thanks especially to my editor Rūta Rimas, without whom this story would have no center; to Tyler Champion, whose illustrations continue to wow me; and to Jessica Jenkins, who is a master of design.

I am also lucky to have a fiercely supportive wolf pack of my own. I won't list them all here, but will certainly call out Dhonielle Clayton and Zoradia Córdova, to whom this book is dedicated, for their friendship, teasing, and encouragement. Thanks also to my family for their continued support of my wild career and to my wife, Tessa, who is always the final reader on any project.

And finally, thank you for reading and for putting this book into the hands of young readers.